The Seed & Other Fairy Tales

Joseph Hillenbrand

First Edition

For more, visit my site:

www.UndertowStories.com

To Jennifer, who encouraged me to come out of my shell.

Illustrations:

Cover & The Seed - Dan Burgess

Unwished - Shannon Toth

The Girl in the Forest - Swee Chin Foo

Two and One - David Procter

Calimire - Jinwoo Kim

My All - Maria Forrester

Hunger Pains - Joseph Hillenbrand

Applebite - Amanda Sartor

Sand Castles - Audran Guerard

Contents:

The Seed

Age 0

Caroline was born with a guardian angel, or rather a guardian ghost. The ghost called herself Rhea and took the form of a thirteen-year-old girl. She was...*mostly* benevolent—always to Caroline, less so to others.

The pregnancy had gone smoothly. Her mother, Hermione, put on some weight during that time, more than usual, but she carried it well. Caroline was birthed at home, with little fanfare. Hermione had spent the previous few months nesting: setting up the crib, decorating the baby's room with trinkets and stuffed animals and such. The farmhouse they lived in wasn't much to look at, but it was home. And now Caroline was finally here. Hermione beamed with a healthy glow as she held her newborn in her arms, and whispered promises of the future.

In the cradle, Rhea would tinkle the mobile of stars and moons that floated above the newborn. Caroline watched closely; her eyes widened and her hands reached to the skies.

Age 1

Caroline's ashy skin garnered some worried looks from the other moms—especially when they compared it to her mother's ruddy complexion. Hermione had quietly ignored all the unsolicited suggestions. "You need to feed her more carrots and sweet potatoes." "She needs to spend more time in the sun." "Is she getting enough vitamin C?" Some would gossip to each other that she needed to lose that baby fat, but Hermione knew the "she" in this case referred to her and not her child. Still, Hermione wasn't embarrassed about her weight. She knew she would lose it over time. She always did.

Although Hermione had a temper, she knew how to hide it around others. In public she was shrinking, nearly invisible. The other mothers and townsfolk thought she was simple, dull. They felt they had the right, even the responsibility, to provide advice; to support her and her child. Yet they didn't *really* care. Most didn't even know her name. Hermione avoided people as much as she could; it was too dangerous to get close. In fact, she had done such a good job that no one could tell you when she had moved in. But most knew where she lived: the small homestead ten miles or so from town as the crow flies; a large plot of land, too large for a single mother to keep up. It was a bit of an eyesore and a breeding ground for tetanus. Old rusted pieces of farm equipment were scattered around. The requisite desiccated truck up on cinder blocks, with weeds and grass growing through the engine block. Nothing grew on the farmland now, as if the soil had been sown with salt. Parents told their children to keep away. A few youngsters were brave enough to venture onto the property, but none stayed too long. They could sense the eeriness, the evil that bled forth from the very ground.

No one saw the inside of their home. Hermione never had friends or family over. It was just the two of them.

Age 2

At age two she started to talk. Not just simple words or phrases, but real sentences. It was quite a dramatic change, as previously Caroline had barely said a word. Up until this point, she had just been taking everything in. Most of her communication had been pointing or simple words. "Eat. Mommy. Baby." Then suddenly this jumped to "Can I have some water?" Her mother was proud, even though her country accent was less pronounced in her daughter; even though it felt as if there was a little less of her in Caroline.

Hermione would bring her daughter little gifts. Barrettes that glinted in the sun. Silver trinkets that were cold to the touch. Some were rewards for being good, or speaking instead of pointing. But those were just excuses. Hermione loved to collect things. The house was littered with items she had scavenged over the years. Each day something new was added, and it would not even last twenty-four hours before it was consumed by the home, forgotten and lost.

Caroline would run and bounce with endless energy. Her mother would toss her high into the air and cry "Fly, Caroline, fly!" Although still a large woman, Hermione kept up with her rambunctious child and was losing weight slowly but surely. Caroline adored her mother and would nest in the crook of her arm while they read picture books together. Oh, yes, she started to read at this age too. "Clever Caroline" her mother would call her. Caroline had no idea she was advanced for her age, as she seldom saw other children, rarely talked to them, and never played with any. Her only point of comparison was her mother and the distance between them always seemed too great.

Her mother took great pride in Caroline's intelligence and growth. It was somewhat ironic, as Hermione did not come across as educated. She lacked a formal education and it came out brutally in her poor grammar and country rube dialect. Yet Hermione had an imposing intellect and wielded it like a weapon—sometimes as sharp as a scalpel and at other times as blunt as a sledgehammer. The problem was, it wasn't directed where people could see it—it wasn't used for some financial gain or academic pursuits—it was all focused on her daughter. Caroline inherited a lot of these same traits and would learn to use her intelligence to defend herself.

However, Hermione didn't deserve all the credit for her daughter's growth. Caroline's spectral friend had an impact on her that was just as big, if not bigger. She would spend time with Caroline while Hermione was in town, or out scavenging.

The two of them played games, read, solved puzzles, and told jokes. Caroline's favorite:

"Knock, knock."

"Who's there?"

"Caroline."

"Caroline who?"

"Caroline *me*!"

And she would scream and jump into Rhea's arms. It was Rhea's favorite too. Sometimes she would tickle Caroline or twirl her high in the air at the end of the joke. But interacting with the physical world was tricky and taxing and she couldn't do it indefinitely. And you know how children like repetition. Caroline didn't understand why Rhea had to stop playing sometimes and disappear entirely, but Rhea always made sure she said her good-byes first.

Age 3

She was a finicky eater and a rail of a girl. Her mother would put all kinds of food in front of her, but she would only nibble. Even filling her plate full of the foods she enjoyed, apples and peanut butter and such, didn't help. "You need to eat. You are all skin 'n' bones." At the same time Hermione would eat like a bird. She was often seen snacking on homemade trail mix and would sup only on salads mixed with berries. Anyone who cared enough to notice would assume Hermione was on a diet to lose weight. But Hermione never really paid much mind to her weight or how she looked. She simply had a very restricted diet. Only certain foods agreed with her, natural foods that she could harvest for free. This regimen caused her to shed pounds whether she wanted to or not. But her daughter did not have the same issues, so there was always the battle around how much food was left on the plate. Eventually Caroline would be forced to finish everything before she could leave the table, but she never put on weight and this troubled her mother.

Sometimes Caroline pilfered some morsels from dinner and brought them to Rhea—not quite understanding that Rhea had no use for them. But Rhea played along and mimed popping the peas or what have you in her mouth, chewing them up good and swallowing them down in a huge gulp, then rubbing her tummy for good measure. This last part always made Caroline giggle in glee.

Age 4

Caroline was a practical girl. When the thistles of the broom fell out, she replaced them with straw from the field. And when the window in her bedroom wouldn't stay up, she found a slat that she would turn up to open the window and then turn flat when she wanted it closed. Her mother fawned over how bright and industrious she was. "Smart as a whip," she would say.

Caroline often grew lonely. She had no siblings to play with. Her mother kept her isolated. No playdates. No family or friends to visit. No speaking to other children. And somehow Hermione was never around either. She was often out in town. Which was odd because she didn't have a job. But Caroline adapted. When she was lonely, she would start to sing. And it wouldn't be long until another voice would join her. Then, at the end of the song, Caroline and Rhea would clap and cheer and start another. Some songs Caroline had learned from her mother and others she made up with Rhea.

♫ Roll yourself away
Roll yourself away
The land will turn to hay
The birds will lead the way
And nothing will be the same ♫

Or another one they enjoyed:

♫ Jesus lay me down
I'll kneel before your crown
The trials fill me deep
And hold me in your keep

So pray so pray the world

For strength to live your word ♫

Rhea encouraged Caroline to think differently. To not take anything too seriously. To question everything.

Age 5

Being homeschooled did not help Caroline's social life. It also didn't really help her relationship with her mother. For every correct answer, Hermione would nod and continue. Every incorrect answer met with disapproving clucks. Caroline learned so many interesting things. Some of which were even true. Of course, Hermione taught some of the basics: math, elementary reading, some science, a lot of religion. But mainly she focused on what she considered essentials: how to identify plants and animals, how to cook, and how to clean. Hermione wanted to make sure her daughter would be useful. Caroline was eager to please. She wanted her mother's approval so much. Hermione knew this and did what she could to encourage that behavior.

However, most of what Caroline learned wasn't from the lesson plans. That attention can be bought but affection must be earned. That what's good for the goose isn't good for the gander. That Peter Pan is for children, but fairy tales are for adults.

Caroline had a second teacher in Rhea. She taught her that there is magic in the world. That there is life in laughter. That tall tales are true.

Age 6

For her sixth birthday, Caroline was promised her own bed. She had spent the previous five years sleeping in a crib that was much too small for her (and had been for some time now). She would have to lie in the fetal position to fit. The crib, like the rest of the house, was covered in gleaming gewgaws and beaming baubles—everything from tinfoil to costume jewelry. Caroline often had a difficult time sleeping alone. She needed to lie next to her mother, often touching her, in order to feel safe enough to sleep. Any time Caroline did manage to fall asleep on her own, Hermione would find some excuse to wake her up, usually something that scared her a bit so she would have to be comforted by her mother. "I'm right here, baby," she would coo softly until her daughter curled into a little ball and slipped back into the land of dreams.

"I don't believe in ghosts, Caroline. And neither should you."

"But she broke the jar."

"No, you broke it. Why are you always lying to me?"

"Sorry, Mommy."

She silently cleaned up the broken pieces of the flour jar under her mother's watchful eye. This was Hermione's special flour—it was darker and coarser than most flour and she used it only on special occasions. And when Caroline tried to use it to bake cookies, Rhea knocked it out of her hands.

While Hermione loomed crunching on an apple—flesh, core, seeds and all—Caroline thought of how she could prove to her mother that ghosts were real. But she wasn't sure that was really a good idea. She wanted to keep Rhea to herself. She was a playmate of sorts. And her mother might try to separate them if she knew what the spirit told her. At times Rhea would get upset and start acting crazy. She would start to yell and destroy things: nothing of Caroline's but things that belonged to her mother. And that's when she would tell on Rhea. "Why should I take all the blame?" she thought.

Dinner was filled with silent reproaches. Caroline wasn't able to leave until she cleaned her plate and then was sent to her room immediately afterwards—a punishment she gladly accepted. She did her math. She read the Bible. She stared vacantly, waiting for sleep. Her eyes grew bleary. Her breath rose louder. Her mind started to dance. Then she heard a familiar voice that snapped her out of this dreary haze.

"Caroline!" Rhea called in a whispered shout. A sense of excitement was woven in her tone. "Come see what I found!"

Caroline hopped out of bed and followed the voice to her closet. Rhea was there, on her knees, hunched over, her back to Caroline. Her face was craned backward, looking even whiter next to her midnight-black hair. If Caroline was pale, then Rhea was translucent. "Look!"

The lower right panel at the back of the closet lay on the ground, exposing a little passageway.

"Where does it lead?"

"Nowhere," Rhea said. "It's a hidey-hole. There's a chest inside. Help me pull it out."

Together they reached into the darkness and dragged it out, inch by inch. The sound of it sliding against the wood floor seemed so loud Caroline feared it would be heard by her mother.

Caroline looked at Rhea for approval before slowly, carefully, cautiously lifting the top up. The lid in and of itself was heavy. The hinge could barely hold it up. In the darkness, she leaned over deeply to peek at the contents while Rhea watched expectantly from behind.

Inside were toys. Dolls, games, cards, stuffed animals—toys she had never seen before but couldn't wait to play with.

"Do you like them, Caroline?"

"Yes."

"Do you love them?"

"Yes."

"Do you love me?"

"Yes."

"Don't tell your mom. She will just take them away if she finds out."

"I won't." Caroline had many questions—about the toys and her mother and Rhea—but did not want to risk missing out on the fun. So she kept them to herself.

There was one toy, though, she did not like at all. An old puppet with a hard wood head and cloth that covered the three sticks used to operate the arms and turn the head. She was too young to recognize the Punch puppet by name and too distracted to notice her initials were carved into it.

The girls played for hours that night in joyous whispers, careful not to draw unwanted attention. But soon enough Rhea had to leave and Caroline went to bed holding a stuffed animal in her arms. She made sure to hide it under her pillow the next morning.

Age 7

"Let's go, Caroline, before it gets dark out."

Caroline sat on the floor, slowly putting on her rubber boots.

They trudged out to the field in stony silence. A lone oak tree decorated the landscape of swaying fields of tall grass. It was a warm fall afternoon. The leaves had turned. Many of them had fallen, making the task at hand all the more difficult. The birds watched carefully. Caroline slogged at a distance behind her mother. The necks of her untied boots flared. Somehow she managed to keep them on the whole time. Hermione stalked around the tree, searching for acorns that had dropped. Caroline took the right side while her mother took the left. She worked quickly, knowing they could not leave until all had been gathered. Each acorn found was put in the bag for some future feast. They had been doing this for as long as they both could remember.

They returned home late. It had gotten dark out. While her mother prepared dinner, Caroline went to her room. Rhea was already there. She could tell Caroline was bothered by something.

"Talk to me. What's going on?"

"I hate this."

"What?"

"I hate scrounging for food. I hate being poor. I hate feeling like a loser."

"Oh, honey. It's just…things are tough right now. It'll get better."

"No it won't. Nobody else lives like this: no car, no food, the house is a mess. I just want to be normal."

"Look, nobody's normal. That's what makes people special. Nobody else knows what it's like to be you. You've learned to fend for yourself. You get to talk to spirits. Just wait, you will turn out stronger and more independent than any of them."

"A lot of good that does me now."

"Sometimes you have to be patient. Sometimes you have to take the long view of things."

Age 8

Caroline sat sobbing in her room. Her breath stuttered delicately as the tears streamed hot and wet from the corners of her eyes.

"Tell me what happened," Rhea said softly, seriously, as she knelt facing her. Caroline said nothing and tried to cry more quietly.

"Did she hit you?"

Caroline nodded twice. Her eyes did not move from the spot on the floor.

"Where?"

Caroline's raised her head, her eyes huge and watery, her forehead wrinkled. Her lower lip quivered as she held her hand to her left cheek, which was clearly redder than the other.

"I'm sorry, Caroline. You don't deserve this. No one should take their anger out on you." Rhea moved to sit next to Caroline and put her arm around her. Caroline felt nothing.

Caroline sat on the back porch, sipping the lukewarm water from her mason jar. The hot night air stuck to her, but she didn't mind. The crickets chirped loudly. They vied for attention with the throaty frogs. She watched the fireflies fade in and out. Using both hands, she tipped the bottom of the jar up high to gulp down the last of the water. She grabbed the lid and focused on one of the soft lights hovering in the field. She neared it, trying to guess where it would reappear each time it vanished. She was patient. And when she was sure, she swooped up the insect into her jar, slapped the lid on it and screwed it on tightly. She pulled out of her pocket an old rusty nail, which she used to poke holes into the lid. It created perfect-size slots: big enough to fit blades of grass through, but too small to let the firefly escape. She grabbed a few long blades of grass nearby and fed them through the perforations. Tucking the jar under her left arm, she sneaked in the back screen door, careful not to let it slam behind her.

She crept into her bedroom and placed the jar on the floorboards next to her bed. She lay down in front of it, hands folded under her chin, watching the tiny insect explore its new home as it crawled up the side of the glass. Caroline flicked the jar where the firefly was. It took to the air and fluttered in place for a second or two before landing. Unsatisfied, she picked up the jar and shook it. It flew again and this time it lit up for a second. She reached under her bed and pulled out the first of three more jars that she kept hidden there. She shook it too and the firefly in this one also took to the air and glowed. But when she took the third jar and shook it, nothing happened. She peered at the bottom of the cool glass container and saw the lifeless firefly. She pulled out the fourth jar, already knowing this one too must be dead, but checking anyway.

Caroline hadn't quite figured out how to keep the fireflies alive more than a day or so. She'd tried different food—leaves, grass, weeds—and even added water once, but nothing seemed to help. Tomorrow she would empty those last two jars out and try again. For the first time since she'd started collecting them, she wondered what the life-span of a firefly was. Maybe they lived only a couple of days. But then she thought that maybe they died of loneliness. She worried about this and considered trying to put two fireflies in the same jar, but decided against it as she was too concerned one or both of them would escape.

Age 9

She loved to take things apart. And sometimes even put them back together again. The toaster was her first victim. And now it had fewer screws and a little more bandaging tape than most toasters its age. Her mother did not find this trait endearing. "This place is fallin' apart fast enough without you helpin' it along." And this was true. Recently the hot water heater had been acting up. The pilot would go out from time to time and Caroline would relight it. But one night she couldn't get it lit again.

She shut off the gas and tried replacing the thermocouple with one that Hermione had found in the local junkyard, but that didn't work. Hermione refused to have someone come in and fix it, so they boiled water on the stove or, if it was summer, outside over the fire pit. They would take sponge baths when needed. When their clothes became too dirty or had lice, they would fill a steel garbage can with water and bring it to a boil, then dump in their laundry and stir it with a long stick. Caroline was humiliated. She always felt as if people were watching, even though the nearest neighbor was acres away.

But this was the only way Caroline would learn—through trial and error. This autodidactic approach became a necessity when her mother stopped homeschooling her (not to mention that there were no books in the house other than the Bible). Hermione felt Caroline knew the basics. Teaching her anything beyond that was as pointless as teaching a pig to sing. But Caroline still had a desire to learn. She wanted more out of life than just this run-down farm.

Age 10

Caroline didn't respond. She didn't want to hear it so she sat in silence and pretended it hadn't been said.

"I won't be here forever," Rhea warned. "And even if I were, I couldn't protect you from everything. So listen carefully: the next time you go into town, I want you to talk to the old woman at the general store. She can help you."

It took a while, but eventually Caroline was allowed to join her mother when she went to town for supplies. Maybe it was the stress or maybe it was her diet, but the flushed color had slowly faded from Hermione, making her appear more stoic. And the locals also took notice of Hermione's weight loss and would have complimented her on it if they had felt comfortable enough to approach her. As it was, Hermione walked with her head held a little higher than usual.

And while her mother waded through the aisles of oats and grains, Caroline made a beeline for the elderly woman who worked the cash register. She slunk up to the counter, which came up to her chin. The old woman leaned over slowly, resting her right arm on the wooden top that had been made smooth by all the hands that had come across it over the years. The woman leaned in aggressively.

"I had a dream about you," she said. Her left hand tried to point at Caroline, but the years weighed heavy on her and her arm could not keep from shaking. "You walked in here with another girl—one a little older than you. She asked that I give you something. You wait here." She waddled off to the back room, looking every bit like a woman who needed a cane. After a minute she came back out, carrying a tiny pillbox in her right hand. Resuming her place behind the counter, she set down the box and flipped open the top.

"When you feel too big, you know, take this and you will become small." She pointed to the brown pill in the spot reserved for Monday. "And when you feel too small, eat this." this time she nodded toward the yellow Saturday pill. The pills looked funny. They reminded Caroline of seeds—cypress and lotus seeds, to be exact.

Age 11

"You're being selfish."

"But it's my money."

"You know how showy that is. How that reflects on me. You know, Caroline."

"It's just an iPod, Mom. Everyone has one."

"You think you're so special in that red dress. It's not always about what you want."

"Right, like how I can't ever have friends over."

"You know we can't have people over. You know what would happen."

"What? Nothing is going to happen, Mom. And even if that were possible, it's easy enough to fix. We'll just throw stuff out."

"You can't just throw things out! We need them."

"Mom, they're worthless."

"Fine, I see how much you care about me. But when Child Services come and take you away from me and everything goes to hell, it will be your fault and you will have to live with yourself."

The house started to shake. Pictures fell and the floorboards started to pull away from the walls. Caroline's tears dripped slowly from her cheeks as she went upstairs to her bedroom. She slammed the door behind her.

"I don't want to hear one peep from you, Caroline!" Hermione squawked. "Not one peep!"

The winters were unforgiving, cold and harsh and rife with snow. They seemed to be getting worse each year. The snowstorms were more frequent and more powerful. The temperatures dropped lower and lower. At times the two of them would be housebound. The snowdrifts would cover the windows on the west side of the house where Caroline's room was. When she was younger, her mother would start a fire and they would roast marshmallows over it while sipping from steaming mugs of hot chocolate. To pass the time they would play board games or cards. But things had changed over the years. These days they went to their separate rooms. Hermione usually took long naps and came out only to make herself dinner. Caroline would sit in her room reading. If Rhea was around, Caroline would talk to her about her dreams. They made up stories and plays and then acted them out.

One winter's day Caroline decided to head into town, behind her mother's back, to get that iPod she wanted. It was roughly ten miles. She figured that the round trip would take over six hours. If she left early in the morning, three hours before the store opened, she could be back before her mother woke up, or at least before she came out of her room. Snow still remained from the previous storm, but it was only a couple of inches deep. The temperature was barely in the teens, but she knew it would warm up when the sun rose. She figured this was as good as it would get until spring. So she headed out. The snow was pristine, as if just fallen. She crunched her way across the field, leaving clear tracks that she hoped she would not have to explain to her mother. When she was about halfway there, the wind picked up and the sky began to darken. The temperature dropped as the first few snowflakes began to swirl in the air. Her feet had gone from cold and wet to frozen and tingling. She was starting to worry about frostbite. It began to snow harder and the wind howled straight at her, making each step more difficult, more dangerous. Caroline was beginning to second-guess herself. She wasn't sure she could make it safely into town but she already passed the point of no return. If she couldn't make it, how would they find her? The snow had already covered up her tracks and her mother didn't know where she was or where she was going. She wanted to stop and try to warm her feet, but she knew that was a bad idea. So she kept on. It took almost twice as long as she'd thought. When she made it to the Walmart, she took off her boots and rubbed her feet vigorously until some feeling came back. It was an unpleasant burning feeling, but at least it was something. She purchased the iPod with the little money she had (and a little of her mother's money too). She waited a bit for the storm to die down before trekking back home.

Caroline was lucky to make it back before her mother woke up. But secrets did not keep in that house and it wasn't long before Hermione found the iPod hidden under her pillow. Hermione stuck a paper clip in the headphone jack, trying to break it, but managed only to make the sound come out staticky. Once done, she put it back where she'd found it.

Age 12

The cold air brought out the red in Caroline's cheeks as she bounded along. She had been told there were wolves in this forest. That she should be careful. She had heard howls from time to time, but had never seen one. Until this day. He was about twenty feet off. His mouth slathered in a greedy smile. He was slowly circling her, steadily moving one paw at a time. She was intimidated by his great size, his black coat, and the sharp teeth that he bared readily. Yet Caroline knew something was off. Wolves typically traveled in packs. She wasn't sure what to make of it.

She knew better than to run, but she couldn't help herself. She couldn't tell if the wolf was chasing her; she never looked back, but she swore she heard his panting in her left ear, and felt the warmth of his breath on her neck.

Caroline knew to expect blame rather than sympathy from her mother. She imagined the phrases that would be thrown at her. "You shouldn't've gone by yourself." "You're too young." "I can't trust you to do the simplest of things." So she talked only to Rhea about it. Rhea was always there with a gentle word. She knew when to offer advice and when to listen. That's all Caroline needed—someone who didn't think she was insane.

With the back of her wrist Caroline wiped off the sweat that beaded on her forehead. She was careful not to get any of the dirt from her soiled work gloves on her. The sun was high. It was a hot day for spring. The thermometer said eighty-five degrees, but it felt more like ninety. She stood for a second, stretching. Her back was sore from bending over so much. She had decided to plant crops—potatoes, broccoli—just enough for the two of them, but still, it was a lot of work. She squinted, hands on hips, her white T-shirt smudged with brown dirt. The knees of her jeans were completely black. She stared at the expanse. The vastness of the land was overwhelming at times. The dry, brown, rippling waves of soil went on for acres. To the west they ran on until they reached a small grassy hill where the acorn tree stood as a lone sentinel. She gazed, silently admiring the achingly beautiful desolation that lay ahead of her.

She didn't think much would grow. The land was too dry and she doubted there were enough nutrients left in it. She was worried that the years of neglect might have made the land unusable. The birds had kept their distance. Even the insects that had been ever present when she was a child had seemed to disappear. She remembered how loud the nights used to be, but these days there was a solemn quiet. She thought of how her mother had once used this very plot of land to plant her garden too. It was funny: her mother's hands were more bruised and scabbed over now than they had ever been back then—back when she was actually working. But that had been years ago and the land had since atrophied. Now Caroline just had to wait for rain and hope. They couldn't afford fertilizer and all the tilling and planting had to be done by hand. She had heard of some farms where they burned down the stalks left behind after the harvest. This was usually done in spring, right before planting. Some said it was to help fertilize the soil, others believed it prevented weeds, and still others did it to drive out insects and disease. She had vivid memories of the first time she had seen it. The ground was black with seared twigs and ashy soil. And amid the charcoal loam grew a solitary blade. Tall and fresh and green, it stood in defiance against its surroundings.

Age 13

Caroline was nervous. She was nervous because Rhea was in her mother's bedroom. She was nervous about saying to Rhea that she was nervous. Although Caroline had caught up to Rhea in age, at least appearance-wise, Rhea was still in charge. Her mother kept her bedroom locked and had warned Caroline to keep out. "It's only for grown-ups," she had said. Rhea was immune to the natural laws and was able to open the door as she pleased.

"I'm not coming in," Caroline declared as she stood at the doorway, feet together, arms folded. She was shivering a little, but this might have been a result of the furnace being broken.

"Oh, please. It will only take a minute. You don't even have to touch anything. Just look."

Caroline leaned deeply over the threshold. Her dark eyes peered over rosy cheeks into the room, toward the top of the bed, where the voice had come from. She couldn't see anything. Not what she was looking for, anyway. She leaned back, closed her eyes, and listened for any sound of her mother returning home. Then, after inhaling a little more heavily than usual, she gently stepped into the room.

She had to tiptoe around and over the piles of her mother's "treasures." There were a few spots where she could see the floor through the stockpile of junk that had value only in Hermione's mind. This room was maybe even worse than the others. Empty soda cans, jars of her mother's special flour, boxes filled with paper clips, binders, papers yellow with age, rusted pans, and more made up this bizarre obstacle course. Caroline seemed to remember a time when the house hadn't been like this, but she couldn't be sure.

Rhea sat cross-legged on the bed. A faint smile crossed her lips as she saw Caroline. "Take a look at this," she said as she lifted the pillow up. The kitchen blade gleamed in a crooked, rusty smile as it lay exposed on the bed.

"Why would my mom keep a knife under her pillow?" Caroline thought aloud.

"That's a good question."

"What do you know about this? Did you put this here?"

"No, Caroline." Rhea's tone had an undercurrent of pity.

Caroline thought for a moment. She looked to the right of the bed, where a bunch of papers were piled high. There lay a picture frame. Inside was a picture was of her mother, much younger-looking, smiling, happy. She was full of life and almost unrecognizable as the person Caroline knew now. She scanned the room for more photos or albums, but there were none. All of a sudden, this struck her. Why were there no photos of her? She never saw any childhood photos, or any type of memorabilia for that matter. No baby boots, no drawings, no handmade cards for her mother. No, none of these things existed anymore. It was odd for someone who kept everything. Caroline felt as if she had no past. As if she didn't matter. As if she didn't exist.

"We should go," she said to Rhea.

From that point on, Caroline started to become suspicious. Suspicious of everyone.

The next night at dinner she decided to investigate. "Mom, I was thinking about Dad."

"Men are no good, Caroline," her mother's ragged jaw snapped. The corners of her colorless mouth had begun to droop, giving her a perpetual frown. With age her nose had grown longer and sagged downward. The loss of weight had turned her once-round chin sharp, beaklike. The dry pale skin made all her expressions severe. "That's why I told you over and over to stay away from boys. They're nothing but trouble."

"Why won't you ever tell me anything about him?"

"You're too young, Caroline."

"I'm almost an adult."

"Not yet you're not. Until then, all you need to know is that he left us when you were born."

"But what was he like? What was his name?"

"What does that matter?"

"I want to know where I came from."

"You came from me."

"But Mom…"

"Enough, Caroline! Enough!"

Caroline backed down. She knew her mother was serious, and had seen enough wraths in her time to know she didn't want to see another one.

That night Rhea had a serious talk with Caroline.

"It will happen soon. Maybe even tonight. You can't trust Mom anymore. It's you or her. So keep your pills with you and use them wisely."

"What are you talking about? And why did you call her Mom?"

"Caroline, she's going to kill you. And then she is going to eat you."

"That's crazy!"

"She's an ogre, Caroline. She feeds on us."

"You're not making any sense. There's no such thing as ogres."

"Call it what you will, but she is evil and she's coming after you."

"You still didn't tell me why you called her Mom. And what do you mean by 'she feeds on *us*'? Are you trying to co-opt my life?"

Rhea sighed. "You're not the first. You're not even the first Caroline—that's my name too. When I was your age, our mother cut my throat in the middle of the night as I slept. Then she stored my body in the root cellar and fed on it for weeks."

"What!? Why would you say such horrible things?" Caroline was still confused. She couldn't process all this new information at once.

"It's true. And you have many sisters that have gone before you. She feeds on her children to keep herself young. She's been doing this for decades, maybe even centuries." She paused. "I wish I could do more." Rhea's eyes met Caroline's with all the hope and desire and sadness that could not be expressed in words. "I wish I were real—you know, *alive*. I wish I could fix everything. But I can't. All I can do is warn you."

"I don't believe it. Mom may not be perfect, but she would never *kill* me."

"Why would I lie, Caroline?"

"Because you want me for yourself."

"Caroline, even if I wanted to, I couldn't take care of you." A horrible expression of pain flashed across Caroline's face. She was usually so good at hiding her feelings. "That didn't come out right. What I mean is you need to be able to take care of yourself."

There was a long silence that felt even longer before Caroline replied, "I never want to see you again." Her face was placid. Her voice emotionless. Her eyes empty.

Caroline tossed and turned all night. The slightest of noises roused her from her fragile sleep.

And then it happened.

The floorboards outside her room creaked. The doorknob twisted slowly—so slowly—careful not to make a sound. The door swung open like a ravenous maw. The dark figure cast a long shadow. The only color existed in the knife she held, with its red smile and promises of pain. Caroline held her breath as her mother stealthily glided across the floor, barely making a sound. Her arm rose and fell quickly, powerfully, skillfully. She would have easily killed her daughter in one blow, had she been there.

Caroline struggled not to cry as she hid in her bedroom closet. She watched as her mother threw off the sheets to reveal the gutted pillow. Caroline could feel her mother's rage as Hermione stared down at the slashed pillow, with feathers strewn about. So now all the cards were on the table. Caroline knew her mother was trying to murder her. Hermione knew Caroline was on to her. Caroline could hear the blood thump in her ears as her heart raced. She was worried her mother could hear it too, even though she knew this was irrational. She kept as still as she could while her mother tried to straighten things up. Hermione stuffed the stray feathers back into the pillow and covered it up with the sheets. Caroline watched anxiously, peering through the whitewashed slats of the closet door, for what seemed like an eternity. Finally, her mother pounded out of the room much less quietly than she had entered.

The next morning her mother made Caroline a large breakfast—three eggs, pancakes, toast, ham, sausage, and fruit. They both pretended nothing had happened the night before. Caroline ate cautiously, silently. She furtively glanced back and forth. The bags under her eyes made her seem so much darker than usual. And now her pink skin had faded to a pasty white. For the first time, she looked like her mother's child. Hermione watched hungrily, with blood-red cracked lips that flashed starkly against her pallid face.

"Let's go. Time to work. We need firewood."

The walk to the forest was quiet. There was no need to talk. Each knew what the other thought. Each wanted the other dead.

They reached the clearing at the edge of the forest. They had found a fallen tree a few days ago that they had hauled to this open area. Hermione harvested the wood as she needed it.

"You find kindling while I chop the firewood."

Caroline sighed, pulled her iPod out of her backpack, put in the earbuds, and headed into the woods. Even with the distorted music blasting she could hear the thwacks of the ax splitting the tree and the conking of the wood hitting the ground. Some of the ground was still wet from the rain a couple of days ago, but the land that was a bit higher would provide drier twigs. She started uphill, following a narrow dirt path now covered with leaves. The barren tree branches appeared black against the patchwork of the dull blue-gray overcast sky. They lurched over her as if slowly closing their grip. She sloshed through little puddles, muddying her shoes and leaving wet tracks. Upon reaching the top, she saw a pile of twigs a little bit ahead on the downslope. She trod carefully, leaning back a little with each step, as this side was much steeper than the other. When she was within reach of the pile, she started to crouch down, but the ground slipped away and she tumbled through the twigs into a pit. She landed roughly, but luckily no real damage was done. Her heart was pounding, her mind flickering. She knew it was a trap laid out for her. The hole she was buried in was rather small, but deep enough that she couldn't climb out. She tried to formulate a plan. But she had to hurry, for the chopping sounds that had been as steady as a heartbeat suddenly stopped.

♫ Jesus lay me down
I'll kneel before your crown
The trials fill me deep
And hold me in your keep ♫

Hermione's singing had a Southern twang to it. It hung in the air lazily, hauntingly. She climbed up the hill steadily, her ax gripped tightly with both hands, her knuckles bulging out as if they would break through her weathered skin. Her hands were just as rough and cracked as the ax handle they choked. She kept on moving. Her steps deliberate. Her posture stiff. Her frame skeleton-like, though not frail. No, she was sturdy. Wiry. Dangerous. Her face was stoic but her eyes had the madness of desperation in them.

♫ So pray, so pray the world
For strength to live your word ♫

Hermione stopped singing when she reached the pit she had dug the night before. Her eyes blazed as she stared down into the empty ditch. Well, not completely empty—Caroline had left her backpack and iPod. Hermione couldn't understand how Caroline had gotten out. The pit was too deep to escape from. Even she had needed a rope tied to a tree to climb out.

Tracks. There must be tracks. She had seen a few of them on the way up here. She stooped around, bobbing left and then right, looking for a trace.

"Caroline! Caroline! Come out, Caroline!"

Her voice was sweet and playful, as if they were in the middle of a game of hide-and-seek. She continued to hunt, down one path and up another.

♫ We know the flesh is weak
Your strength, O Lord, we seek
To shed this mortal coil
Reborn in earthly soil

So pray, so pray the world
For strength to live your word ♫

Caroline heard the singing and the calls from her mother, but did not move. Having taken the first pill, she was now no larger than your thumb. The whole time she never left the ditch; she simply hid under a leaf. She hoped to outlast her mother. That at some point her mother would give up and go back home and Caroline could focus on how to escape.

"Caroline, why must you make everything so difficult?" Hermione's tone became agitated. Her hands appeared longer, thinner, sharper. They would tighten and relax their grip on the ax, as if they were breathing. Her dress was soiled with mud and muck and stuck to her legs. Her stringy hair poured down the front of her face.

"Damn it, Caroline! Why is this always about you? I need you to stop being a little bitch and come here!"

Hermione stopped for a moment. She stood up straight and listened—nothing. She cawed twice. All the magpies in the nearby trees looked her way. "*Find her*!" she screamed. They took to the air, turning the sky into furious black and white.

The fever pitch frightened Caroline—the beating of wings, the cacophony of screeches, the pressure of the air—and she shivered beneath the leaf blanket. This little movement was enough to draw the attention of one of the magpies and it swooped down toward her. In one smooth motion it clutched her with its talons and plucked her from the leaf with its beak. It swerved around, switching direction with a panicked Caroline dangling precariously. Hermione seethed as she watched the bird glide to her. "What have you *done*!?" she exclaimed, fearing that eating this tiny version of Caroline would not satisfy her hunger. "You've gone and ruined everything again! Thirteen years wasted. How am I supposed to get young again if you're so small? Look at you. You're the size of my thumb. I'll be lucky to get a year back." Hermione sighed and mumbled the next part more to herself than to Caroline. "Maybe next time I'll have twins to make up for it."

The magpie landed on Hermione's shoulder and she turned her head and tilted it back slightly. "What's done is done." The bird fed Caroline to her mother. Hermione swallowed her daughter whole.

Caroline landed in Hermione's horrid belly. Nothing good could be said of it. All empty, shriveled, black, cancerous, moldy, and smelly. But she wasn't afraid; she had prepared for this moment. "This is it," she thought, and reached into her pocket, pulled out the other pill and swallowed it. She closed her eyes. "It's over now."

Hermione's face started to twist. She felt sick. Her spindly talons clutched at her distended belly. She clawed at her stomach savagely, but it was too late. Caroline burst forth from her mother, red and messy and new. She left behind an empty shell in her wake. But Caroline was different: she was fully grown—an adult. The pill had not only made her physically larger, but aged her as well.

And only now is her tale ready to begin.

Unwished

Heather awoke bleary-eyed and dreary-dreamed. She stumbled into the bathroom, intent on scrubbing that morning breath out of her mouth. Toothpaste foamed and fizzed and she reached for her cup to rinse. As it filled with tap water, she saw a frog float to the top. Speaking softly and seriously, she said, “I think I know just what to do with you.

“What a beautiful bauble you will make,” she said as she tied the frog into her hair. Quickly she got clad, and dashed out the door.

As she clumped her way to the car, through the blustery wind and billowing rain, the frog became concerned for its well-being and begged:

“Please set me free, and I will grant you anything you wish.”

“I have no need for wishes,” Heather responded matter-of-factly. The frog shivered as she kept walking.

To her dismay, Heather saw she had left her car windows open the night before and the Honda was filled with rain—and something else. Something that shimmered in the water. She stooped over and poked her head through the driver’s side window and saw that in the water swam tiny goldfish.

“Save us!” they exclaimed.

“From what?” she asked.

“We have nothing to eat,” they explained.

“Oh, *I see* something,” she said, remembering how delicious she found fishes.

"Please, no. Set us free and we will grant you a wish."

"I have no faith in wishes from fishes," she said. "They never come true. But I have a great idea. Since today is too lovely to go to work, why don't we all go on a picnic instead?"

Heather dipped into the car through the window, careful not to let any fish out, and drove to the park, slish-sloshing all the way.

When they arrived, she scooped up all the fish into a blender she kept in her trunk for just such emergencies.

She walked and walked (and walked some more), looking for a place to set up her blanket and basket and blender and bread and barbecue until she tripped over a rabbit's hole. Angry that she had almost broken her ankle, she stomped on the opening, trying to tamp it shut.

"Please stop or you will bury me here," begged the rabbit. "If you leave me be, I will grant you a wish."

"Wishes are nothing but trouble," complained the girl. "But I meant no harm to your home. I had no idea someone lived here. Come, join my picnic, and we will have a wonderful time." The rabbit found this quite acceptable and joined her party.

Heather sat down on the square checkered blanket she laid out.

The fish chummed on her right.

The frog croaked to her left.

The rabbit stewed in front.

What a nice little meal she had of cuisses de grenouille, hasenpfeffer, and fish smoothie.

Just as she began to eat, the coworker she had a crush on happened to walk by.

“What are you doing here, Mike?” she asked.

“Playing hooky,” he replied.

“Me too! Won’t you join me for lunch?” she offered. Mike smiled as he sat down next to her and crossed his legs.

She mirrored his smile.

“If you had one wish, what would it be?” she asked.

The Girl in the Forest

He awoke with a start.

The pounding of his heart drowned out all other sounds.

BUM bump. BUM bump. BUM bump.

Savagely it beat.

BUM bump. BUM bump.

His head was heavy.

BUM bump.

He couldn't breathe.

BUM bump.

His throat was completely clogged.

BUM bump.

Clogged full of something solid and weighty.

BUM bump. BUM bump.

And sputtering from his lips was a weak, whimpering cough.

BUM bump. BUM bump. BUM bump.

He was suffocating. Dying. Buried alive from the inside out. He tried to dig himself from this shallow grave; thrusting his fingers into his mouth he was able to hollow out a passageway. The detritus he had excavated turned out to be stones of indiscriminate shapes and sizes. Some were smooth and oval, others rough and craggy. They varied in size too, from as large as a walnut to as small as a pea. But before he could grab another handful, more rocks spewed from his stomach, pushing through his throat and into his mouth, replenishing the ones he had just removed. He tried again and again, but try as he might, he could not keep his mouth clear—the stones always came back. It seemed futile.

So he stopped trying.

He clenched his jaw and sealed his lips. This seemed to stifle the flow of stones. His chest burned and his coiled stomach ached from coughing. The jagged rocks stretched his esophagus and cut the insides of his cheeks. He still couldn't breathe. Panic swelled. He had to do something. "Relax," he told himself. He tried to slow down his racing mind by focusing on just one thing—breathing. He took a long, measured, deep breath. The air snaked around the stony obstructions and trickled into his lungs until they were completely full. Slowly he exhaled.

Each breath was a tense struggle for life.

Inhale...exhale...

In...out...

Again...and again...

This seemed to work, but he needed to be patient. Eventually he set his breathing to a rhythm, and it comforted him a little. But he knew he couldn't live like this. He needed to find a cure. So he got out of bed, headed downstairs, out the back door, and into the ready forest, where the answers lie.

***

Past the briars and the thistles and the brambles, in a small clearing near a cabin, she sat—waiting. A pack of dogs surrounded her. One of the smaller ones sat in her lap, enjoying the attention. The others prowled around her restlessly, jealously. In front of her, on the forest floor, lay an ornate box, glowing from within. There was something different about her; she emanated an aura of power. He recognized it immediately, but could not put a name to it.

“I see you noticed my tinderbox. No doubt curious what’s inside,” she said to the traveler. “Yes—well, it’s locked and I haven’t the key anymore. I’m not sure I would even recognize the contents—it’s been such a long time.”

She found she was lost for a moment.

“Anyway, you obviously want something from me or you wouldn’t be here,” she complained as she pushed the dog out of her lap. It turned and tried to make its way back, while the others looked on expectantly, hoping to take the fallen’s place. “Shoo!” She gave it a kick to show she meant business. “Get!” They all retreated to the perimeter.

“So?” she asked with a hint of impatience.

He smiled, showing more rocks than teeth. “Hmm…“ She stood, letting her long golden hair flow in the wind, and neared him to get a better look. She plucked one rock out only to see another gurgle forth.

“Yes, I’ve seen this.” She softly reached out in an action that was both bold and timid. The tips of her slender, delicate fingers caressed his midsection. He didn’t know how to react. “I have no feeling in my fingertips,” she offered. “The nerves end just short.” She flattened her palm against his abdomen and applied pressure. “Ah, there it is. You have a large stone in your stomach. It keeps you grounded, tethered. But it grows too large—the edges break off and bubble up to your mouth and *that* is what you are seeing.” She smiled sheepishly and removed her hand. “You can live this way for a while, but it will get worse and eventually you will become completely sedentary.

“I think I can help you. But first you must help me.” She circled him as she spoke, making sure to brush against him accidentally from time to time. “There are three beasts in the forest, each of which has an item of mine. Retrieve the items for me. Go to the east and find the wise old owl—he possesses the first. Then there is a cabin by the lake which is home to a fox and the second item. And finally, in the heart of the woods is a den where the king of the forest and the last item can be found. Do this for me and I will grant your wish.

"In the meantime, you can use this." She handed him a small vial of liquid. "It will stop the rocks from forming—only for a little while, but at least you will be able to talk. It is very rare and all I have, so use it wisely."

***

It took some time, but he finally found the owl perched on an oak tree branch about ten feet off the ground. He cleared his mouth of any stones and took a sip from the vial.

"Mr. Owl, the girl in the forest sent me to retrieve an item of hers."

"Who?"

"I don't know her name."

"Well, now, neither do I," the owl replied petulantly. "What is this item then?"

"I don't know, sir."

"Yes, well, I can see you are woefully inchoate and I am quickly losing interest. I cannot be bothered with this inanity. Now if you don't mind, I must return to my studies."

"Studies?"

"Yes, studies. I am sure you are unfamiliar with the concept." Silence. "You see, I watch these rodents in an effort to decipher their patterns. One must understand one's enemy to be successful. The hunt is mostly preparation. The kill is much too quick and the unprepared will fail. Patience and planning are the key. Now if you don't mind, leave me to it."

"But...the item..."

"Quiet! What could I possess that she could possibly want? I own nothing."

"But...the girl..."

"The girl? Let me tell you about the girl. She was left as a babe at the root of my tree. I taught her everything she knows: about trees and animals, about the sun and the moon. About what berries can be eaten and what leaves should not be touched. She learned quickly and left just as quickly. And I have not seen her in all the years since. Now, if you please..." There was a moment of silence while the traveler chose his reply.

"You talk of enemies. Do you consider me your enemy?"

"Enemy? You? You are just an errand boy. A simple, ignorant, and unrefined child."

"Then I submit myself to you. Teach me."

"There is *so* much knowledge I can grant you but I have not the time to cover it all. Nor you the mental capacity."

"Then start with something simple. Tell me about the prey you are studying."

"Hmm...simple..." The owl studied him for a moment. "Well," he said finally, "you see that white mouse over there—straight ahead—looking for food? Each day, at this time, he will spend thirty minutes doing precisely that."

The man launched himself at the mouse, trapping it in his cupped hands.

"What are you doing? I wasn't done studying that specimen."

"I just wanted to present it to you has a gift."

The owl swooped down and snatched the mouse out of his hands. He landed on the ground with more grace than you would expect from a bird of that size.

"It would be rude to refuse a gift." He ate it greedily.

"Teach me more."

"That chipmunk, it is stockpiling goods for the upcoming winter. He will need sixty more grams to have enough."

He stepped on the chipmunk's tail. Then he picked it up, walked over to the owl and dangled the wriggling creature over his head. The owl craned his neck and swallowed the chipmunk whole as it dropped into his waiting maw.

"And that rabbit?"

"He will constantly nibble at vegetation throughout the day. If that is gone, he will strip the bark off of the trees. But this prey is most elusive. He zigs and zags unpredictably. The key is to..."

A knife flew through the air, stopping the rabbit. He gathered the creature. Peeling off its hide he fed the raw meat to the expectant owl.

"Mmm...quite delectable. But now the lesson is over and I must say adieu." He flapped his wings and tried to ascend, but failed. "It appears I have more than sated myself and my carriage cannot be conveyed by my wings. Ah, but the matter will rectify itself soon enough."

He felt the stones rise to the back of his throat. "You have such a beautiful mind," he said as he readied the knife.

***

"*I* have something of *hers*!?" snarled the fox. She paced back and forth, building up her ire. "Really? If anything she has something of mine. I gave her everything she has." She paused and gathered herself.

"She wouldn't have any clothes
Without me
Or food
Without me
She wouldn't know to sew
Without me
Or cook
Without me
And then she left
Without me."

She crooned on softly, gushing self-pity and melodrama.

"And now I grow old
And she is so young
And my looks fade away
And she has the eye of everyone
And my eyesight fails
And she sees others
And who'll care for me
Now that for her I am too much bother?"

"I can't tell you that," he replied (having already sipped from the vial). "My only concern is completing my quest. The owl didn't seem to know what she wanted either."

"Oh, you talked to him, did you? Tsk. Tsk. Tsk.

"He is just as useless as the rest
Wasting time as he hides in his nest

"She arrived at the foot of his tree
And soon he sat her down on his knee
Where he armed her with the ABCs
But then she headed out to be free
And she followed her nose here to me

Since nobody came before his studies

"I should know

"She left me for the boar
And 'twas still not enough
She left the boar for more
Wallowing through the trough
It could all be so easy
But she prefers it rough

"And so now you come
Like a knight in white shining
To save the damsel
Who doesn't want a twining."

"My, what a sharp tongue you have. But I think you are wrong about her. I will get what she requested and she will help me as promised."

"All these ideas you believe to be true
Are silly and naïve, just like you

"She hides behind lines
And speaks only in riddles
Surrounded by lies
The truth stands in the middle."

Her eyes started to gleam as she focused sharply on him.

"Think you're
The first?
The one?
The last?
You are
Nothing
Just like
The rest."

"Maybe, but you can't know that for sure."

"When she sees the you you are
  past the twice-locked door
Will she show the she she is?
  Will she hide it more?"

She pronounced her words more crisply while forcing herself to slow down, to not get too excited.

"I had a dream last night
And you were in it too
And what I thought I thought
And what you thought I knew
That the secrets you keep
All come bleeding through."

"I have no secrets," he retorted.

"Ah, but that's what you seek to hide
That you are ever empty inside
And with a lifetime of nothing
To show—how can you have any pride?"

He took the awkward lull in the conversation to look around (for he could not bear to make eye contact). The cabin was fully furnished, including sofas and chairs and cabinets and dishes and foodstuffs. Not at all the abandoned mess he had envisioned. "Who lives here?"

"*I* do," the fox replied, pausing to emphasize her disdain. "You're not very bright, are you, boy?" She reverted to prose. It felt came across an insult. As if he were not worth the effort to keep up the rhyme.

"I guess not. Have I done something to offend you?"

"No, you are but a puppet on a fool's errand. But since you have imposed yourself as a guest, I suppose I should offer you something to eat. Fetch me that bowl from the top shelf. I haven't been able to reach that for years." He made his way into the kitchen and easily reached the bowl under her watchful eye.

"Please, let me make it. What would you like? Maybe some curds and whey?"

"Yes. It has been a while since someone made me food."

He took the milk and mixed in the vinegar, then strained it into the bowl. And when he was sure she wasn't looking, he added some baking soda. Carefully he presented to her the half-full dish, laying it gently on the cabin floor.

"This smells a bit off," she said, sniffing around the saucer before tentatively slipping out her tongue to taste it. Immediately she cringed and tried to retract it, but the glue gripped her greedy tongue, binding it to the bowl. "Wha?" She slowly backed away into the shadowed corner of the cabin, with the bowl dragging across the wooden floor making a low and steady hollowing sound.

"Here, let me help you with that."

The stones started to shoot out of his throat and clink against the back of his teeth. They were getting sharper and now scratched and cut his insides. His jaw clenched. His lips creased into a smile.

***

Before entering the den he took another swig of the serum. Not bothering to remove the stones, he let the liquid sluice and drip through the jagged rocks. The ones coated in serum slowly disintegrated and he spat them out like watermelon seeds. He strode confidently into the den only to come face-to-face with a giant boar. His tusks full and sharp. His prickly back arched high. He loomed tall, surrounded by countless riches—jewels and gold pieces piled waist-high. Torches hung on the wall, next to trophies of animal heads.

"My lord, I beseech a favor of you. The lady of the forest requests an item that once belonged to her."

"And what? Have you come as her servant? Her bill collector?" The king's voice was so deep and full that he felt it in his bones. His tone was bold, confident. The hint of anger in his voice didn't come across as genuine. It felt like a tactic, a ploy used to make others uncomfortable.

"I come as a man in need."

"Well, you made it further than most. Speaking of which, did you notice those pets of hers? The names on their collars?" The king liked watching his prey squirm.

"A few..."

"Yes?"

"Thomas. James. John."

"Odd names for pets, wouldn't you say? In fact, they sound more like human names."

"Yes."

"And what is your name, human?"

"My name is my own, sire."

"A wise reply. You would be even wiser to keep it from her. Names have power." They stood there, face-to-face, silent and intense, each taking the measure of the other. The boar continued. "As a man, I was a prince and I met her on a hunt. We fell in love but she would not follow me back home. So we stayed in this forest. This land may be smaller than my father's, but I was king here—and I was with her. I kept my kingly duties but she grew bored. And then she was gone—leaving me—with this." The boar lolled his head from one side to the other. His tone had changed. Sadness crept in to dance with anger. "This whole land was ours and she gave it up. She had everything. *What more could she possibly want?* And now, after all that, she sends yet another here asking for something?"

"Obviously, you are a man of power and wealth, but maybe this"—he waved his arm to indicate the den, the riches, the kingdom, and the boar himself—"isn't what she wanted, my lord."

"Watch your tongue or I'll have your head."

"Do you fear me your successor?" he gibed nonchalantly.

"You? Surely you jest. You are merely a slave of the kingdom."

"You should reconsider."

"You *dare?* Bow before your king or *die!*" the beast growled. The creature's heated breath wet its tusks.

"No."

The boar charged at full speed, angry and reckless. He ran out of the den, through the woods, curving through the trees, hoping the largeness of the creature would lessen its agility. It did, but not by enough. The beast would not lose its footing. The hooves beat loudly, shaking the forest, causing all to tremble. Clumps of dirt and leaves flew in his wake. More was needed to encourage a tumble.

He induced the stones to spew forth from his panting mouth. They were covered in blood and painted the ground in a smattering of red. The boar stumbled upon the wet pebbles. It crashed headfirst into a tree, and was dazed long enough for him to get his knife.

***

"Back already? Most don't give up so soon."

The sun was beginning to set, leaving a hazy orange glow in the sky. As he entered her camp, he noticed her pets were nowhere to be found.

He came within two paces of her and presented a satchel still dripping with blood. While she pulled out the contents he drank the rest of the vial.

"Have faith in me," he said. She took a step forward, as did he.

A brain. A tongue. A tusk.

She looked at him with disappointment and fear. "What do you expect me to do with this?" She stepped back.

"Yes, I was afraid that wasn't what you were truly after.

"But do not give up on me. Open the other side." He retreated a step. She lifted the flap and flipped the bag over. Out flopped three hearts.

"Yes." She moved each next to the locked box. The first made the light emanating from the box glow brighter. The second gave the light a reddish hue. The third caused it to pulse. But the effects did not last and it reverted back to the steady, dull white glow.

"It...it didn't work." She trembled on the verge of tears.

"Of course not, what would you expect from these cold, un-beating things? You need to trust me. In talking with these creatures, I realize you have been alone your entire life. As have I.

"You need someone who truly understands you," he intimated.

"There aren't many like us," he explained.

"We need each other, " he insisted.

"But you fail me like the rest. This box is still unopened." She bowed her head to hide her face, allowing the tears to fall straight and silent to the ground. After a long pause to steady herself, she continued. "But you did what I asked and it must not have been easy. Tell me your name so I may grant your wish."

He hesitated before speaking cautiously.

"Kurtis."

"Wren," she said sheepishly.

She put her hand on his stomach for a second time. "Kurtis," she whispered.

It is such a strange feeling to be afraid of your own name.

"Breathe."

He inhaled. She pushed in.

The nausea overwhelmed him and he vomited uncontrollably. He coughed up a large craggy rock mottled with blood and bile. And then he began to lift up off the ground, slowly drifting skyward. She grabbed his hand. He continued to rise until he was completely above her. The scene evoked in him a picture of a little girl holding a balloon.

"The tinderbox," he stammered, "give it to me. Let it replace the stone. Let it be my weight."

"I can't..."

Their eyes met; a flood of emotions flashed between them.

"Don't," he pleaded.

She let go.

He floated away.

***

And forever more, their heads hung low: she afraid to see him again, he unable to take his eyes off of her.

Two and One

Once there was a woodcutter. And one day this woodcutter was in the forest, going about his work, chopping down a tree. As it began to fall, he saw, out of the corner of his eye, a rabbit in the tree's path. Moving quickly, he was able to save the creature from certain doom.

The grateful rabbit said, "You saved my life. And I am in your debt. As a means of repayment, three wishes you get."

Dreams of power and riches filled the woodcutter's head. But before he could respond, he pictured his wife. He cringed visibly. The thought of how she might react if he spent all the wishes himself made him shiver, so he replied, "I gladly accept, but ask that you let me split these wishes with my wife." This way he wouldn't be tempted to use them all himself.

"Easily done. You can have two wishes and your wife can have one."

The woodcutter bade the hare good-bye and set off home.

He found his wife Adeline in the kitchen cooking dinner and told her the good news.

"Oh, Will, how wonderful! We shall have everything we ever desired." Thoughts of diamonds and eternal beauty clouded her mind. "Go sit at the table and we can discuss over dinner."

And so he did, watching her bring out bowls of beet stew. Seeing the best his meager wages could afford, he complained, "Oh, how tired I am of the same meals every day. Just once, I wish I could have something better to eat, like sausage perhaps."

And then, out of nowhere, appeared a two-foot-long sausage, the most delicious thing he could imagine.

"Will, what have you done! Wasting a wish on a sausage!" And before she knew what she was saying, she followed up with "I wish that sausage hung upon the tip of your nose."

No sooner was it said than there was the sausage, hanging down from his nose like an elephant's trunk. This of course, made him quite angry, but seeing his wife sitting across from him, laughing uncontrollably at his plight, doubled his anger, and the only thought that crossed his mind crossed his lips at the same time.

"I wish the sausage hung upon the tip of *your* nose, you ungrateful shrew!"

Just like that, the other end of the sausage attached itself to her nose, binding them together. The smile left her face, as did the anger leave his, both to be replaced with a look of somber despair as they stared with smoldering resentment, realizing they were stuck with each other for the rest of their lives.

Calimire

He made his way through the forest, off one of the trails toward a little pond covered thick with green algae. At least twice a week he came to this spot. It was his respite from work, from deadlines, from people. But today was different. Today he noticed on one of the trees, pinned at about eye level, a piece of paper. As he got closer he could see it was folded in half. And on the outside it bore a single word: his name. He briefly hesitated, looking around to see if anyone was nearby, before he unpinned and unfolded the note. It simply read

"Follow me"

He carefully folded the note back up and made sure the pushpin went through the same hole in the paper, and into the same spot on the tree. And he sat down. And he waited.

The book he had brought along to read was his typical fare—filled with monsters and demons and such—but it couldn't keep his mind from wandering that afternoon.

As the sun started to hide behind the trees, the frogs began to croak louder and faster—at a near-deafening pitch. Out of the murky water rose a beautiful frog woman. Now, frogs are not typically considered attractive creatures (at least not by humans). But she wasn't quite a frog. She was part frog, part human. Not so much like a mermaid, but more of a hybrid. Her eyes were a bit larger and rounder than a human's. Her skin had a greenish glow to it. She had long light-blond hair. And she *was* beautiful.

"You read my note?"

"Yes."

"And you're ready?"

"Yes."

"You know if you leave with me, there is no coming back."

"Yes."

Her throat bulged in a happy, involuntary tic and she smiled broadly, careful not to show any teeth.

He followed her down into the pond. She took his hand, and he felt his whole body tingle. They turned and slowly walked toward the center, sinking with each step, leaving the world in their wake. Fully submerged now, he was able to see a passage toward the other end. She led him toward this underwater tunnel, looking back occasionally with a coy grin, her hair swarming around her face. The tunnel was much longer than he'd thought, and soon he began to run out of air. He wasn't sure how much farther it was, but he knew going back was not an option. His lungs burned for air and he began to panic. Watching her swim farther away, oblivious to his plight, he began to black out.

***

Her lips formed a seal around his mouth as she breathed life into him. They were still suspended underwater when he regained consciousness. She grabbed his arm and swam the rest of the way with him in tow.

They arose from the pool into a strange land. The sun had gone to rest, giving way to stars that gleamed in the clear night sky. Lightning bugs filled the air, buzzing around, performing their mating dance: quickly stealing your attention with their fiery luciferin only to disappear again. Among the lightning bugs were other insects. But what were they? Butterflies? Fairies? Pixies? It was too dark to tell, but everything seemed possible here.

He inhaled deeply, breathing in this new world full of promise. For the first time in his life, he felt he was home.

"Are you feeling better?" she asked when they finally got completely on dry land.

"Yes."

"Let's get you someplace warm and dry." He didn't know why, but he trusted her completely. It was beyond faith. It was more like fact: unproven and unprovable, but fact nonetheless.

"Where are we?"

"In Calimire." She answered so matter-of-factly that he decided not to follow up with another question like "Where is that?"

They followed the worn dirt path lit casually by lanterns that glowed a sleepy violet hue. Little houses dotted the road. Farther beyond lay a dense forest.

She spoke of many things as they walked in rhythm. How she had been watching him from afar. How his intelligence was wasted. How he should have more power. And how power isn't given, it's taken. He listened and nodded. All the while his head buzzed with replies and questions, but the words choked on the way out. At times his mouth would open as if he were about to speak, but nothing came. And so his hand sealed the cavernous maw for fear of echoing nothing. She eventually caught him in the act and asked, "Why do you do this?" and folded her hands over her mouth, comically imitating the Speak-No-Evil monkey. He gave the only defense he could: "My mouth is a source of shame."

"Don't be silly," she cheerfully reprimanded him. "You have so much to offer. So much more than the rest. Most people don't think before they talk. Remember, you're different from the others—special." He wasn't convinced that was a good thing, but he kept it to himself.

"The stars are so bright here," he uttered in awe, neck craned back, mouth agape.

"There is a story about the how the stars came to be." She told it thusly:

"The god of man was tilling the field. And the day grew long. And the sun would not set. Tired and hot, he snatched the sun out of the sky and crushed it in his hand. The heavens fell dark. Then he cast the fragments of the sun into the air. And those tiny little pieces became the stars you see now.

"And then he slept. A thing he had not done for years.

"His wife, though, the goddess of women, knew he would sleep and sleep and never wake again if things stayed like this: with no sun to shine. So she went out into the night collecting the bits of stars from the sky and molded them back into the sun. Then she hung the sun in the sky, which woke up her husband.

"And each day, for the rest of their lives, they would go through the same routine—him turning day into night and her turning night into day." With that, she gave him a little smile to indicate that she was finished and he should say something.

"I like that story," he started. "It shows the cyclic nature of life: day to day, generation to generation. One day is destroyed and the next is created. I mean, we till the same land our ancestors did and the days are the same for us as they were for them. And like, man is the destroyer and woman is the creator." He continued on in this quick-paced stream of thought and inspiration that kept him talking fast and a little breathlessly. His eyes were shut tight the entire time he spoke. "And there's the struggle of power where the man thinks he is in control but actually, she is in control." He realized he was talking a lot. This made him self-conscious, so he stopped and opened his eyes to gauge her reaction. Her only response was a blank look and a quiet smile.

Soon thereafter, she pointed out a farm in the near distance. "I have a friend that lives there. We can stay in his barn tonight." Upon arriving, they climbed up to the hayloft. The earthy smells pervaded all. They lay side by side for some time without a sound. "I'm OK with silence," she felt the need to say. "Yeah, right," he thought. "*I'm* OK with silence. You find it awkward." She turned toward him. He turned toward her. Her eyes locked on to his. She kissed him softly. "Let's get some rest," she said.

She lilted:

"Tomorrow is a big day."

Her voice slowly started to hush:

"Tomorrow we kill my husband."

Until she whispered:

"Tomorrow we kill the king."

***

"Umm…OK. Seriously?"

"Shhh. Yes, now go to sleep."

But sleep wasn't really an option. His confusion made him mute. He didn't sleep well that night, tossing and turning. And looking over at her peaceful slumber he thought, "How can she sleep so easily? What am I getting myself into?" At one point she woke. Smiling at him, she put her hand in his. Only then did his mind numb and he rested.

***

She arose before the sun.

"Did you have any dreams last night?" she asked, finding him stretching on the ground. He tried to remember his dream before it bubbled up into the heavens to be lost forever.

"I dreamed there was a man. He wore a brown suit with a matching top hat. The sun shone brightly above. The light bothered him, so he reached up and plucked the sun out of the sky. The rays streamed out of his hand as his fingers closed tightly around it.

"The world got dark. His fingers bled red as his fist clenched more and more tightly until he crushed the sun into bits. A dull glow still emanated from his hand.

"Then she came. She was beautiful and mysterious and she walked up to him. She opened his hand and blew the still-glowing dust. The particles collected on the nighttime sky and became the stars.

"They turned around and he put his arm around her as they watched the twinkling show." He finished his story and opened his bleary eyes.

"That's pretty. It sounds like the fairy tale I told you," was all she had to say. He was disappointed that she didn't see that this was different. How it was a story about despair turned into hope. The man destroyed the sun, the symbol of life, and the woman came and rescued him by turning the remains, his shattered dreams and hopes, his pain, into something beautiful, something worthwhile.

"We need to get to the castle before the king awakes," she said hurriedly. Then she continued in an offhand tone, "You know, in some ways, you remind me of him."

"Who?" he asked, not following the quick change in topics.

"The king." He let that go, unsure if it was a compliment or an insult…or both.

"So why do you want him dead?" He almost asked instead, "So why are we killing him?" The thought scared him.

"He's destroying the kingdom."

"What—through war? Oppression?"

"Through inaction. The kingdom is collapsing around him and he does nothing. We are at risk of becoming extinct."

"But don't you love him?"

"He married *me*. I didn't marry *him*. You don't say no to the king.

"Look, I've got to get going," she continued. "I need to be back at the castle before the king awakes. You wait here. I know the man who runs this farm. He is the best farmer in the land and his crops go to the king. I will talk to him and ask him to bring you along when he makes his delivery. He will say he found you in the field and ask the king what to do with you."

"Why can't I go with you?"

"Because it will look suspicious. No one even knows that I have been out all night."

"OK. So then what?" He struggled to keep up.

"Then you will be in the castle and we can start enacting our plan."

"Wait. What plan?"

"I will meet up with you at the castle and give you a vial of poison. When you get the opportunity, put it into his chalice. It will be a quick and merciful death."

"Why can't you do this? Why do you need me? Why would I even get involved?"

"I can't be associated with this. Certain people have…suspicions about me. No one knows you and you know no one. You have no motive. And anyway, you will be searched before you enter the castle."

"So right, yeah, speaking of motive, what is mine again?"

She took his hand in both of hers. "When the king dies, I will become queen. We will wed. And you will be my king."

"But you barely know me. Hell, we don't even know each other's names."

"Not true, John. My name is Felicity and I know you better than you think. We are soul mates, destined to be together. You must have felt it too." And he did. Kind of. But this was too quick. This seemed wrong. Oh, how he wished he could listen to his head instead of his heart at times like this. But the emotions overwhelmed him and the best he could do was let out a nervous laugh. She turned her head slightly and gave a smile that made him crumble.

“I really must go. I will send Mark here shortly.”

***

John had only a few minutes to try to sort things out before Mark came in. He was a big man but not as in shape as you would expect from someone who worked the fields all day. Maybe he had farmhands to do this work, or, God forbid, slaves. John didn’t ask. He didn’t want to know.

“Flick tells me I’m to get you into the castle.” The words spat out of Mark’s thick throat over his long frog like tongue. John noticed that Mark’s skin was a darker shade of green than Felicity’s. He wondered if that was a form of tanning, or just variants in pigmentation.

“Yeah, I guess.”

“Says she’s got big plans for you.”

“Well, you know how she is.”

“Yeah, I do.” This statement had a message to it. And what John read infuriated him. But he would never show it. So they stood there, pretending to have a pleasant conversation, all the while each was trying to figure out how much the other knew. “We go back quite a bit. She’s spent quite a few nights here,” the farmer continued to drive in the point. “You know, we don’t get too many of your kind around here. Humans, that is.”

“But there have been others?” John asked.

“Well, yeah, she’s known a few. You know what I mean, right?”

“No, but I’m starting to get the picture. I guess I should just be happy to be in the team photo. So tell me, what do you know about these others? Good-looking bunch, no doubt.”

"Some of them looked like you, if that's what you mean. But none of them lasted too long. Some of them went back home. Others just disappeared. Word of advice: watch out for yourself. Nobody else will. Know what I mean?"

"Let's get going."

***

John rode in the front of the horse-drawn wagon beside Mark. The ride was mostly silent and completely awkward. The road was bumpy. The wagon wheels were slightly warped. Thc unforgiving wooden bench quickly made him tired from sitting. John would have felt relief when they finally arrived, except he knew things were only going to get worse.

The guards stopped them immediately, looking at the stranger agape and agog. When Mark explained the visitor was a human, a sense of hostility filled the air. It made John nervous. Of course, everyone from Calimire was aware of humans, but few had actually seen one. Mark relayed his story dutifully, with sufficient detail and conviction to convince the guards. This scene repeated itself several times, with higher- and higher-ranking officers. Eventually they got to talk to an adviser of the king.

"So how did you get here again?" Malakai the grand inquisitor and advisor to the king asked, trying only slightly to hide his suspicion.

"I found him in the fields when—" Mark tried to explain when he was interrupted by Malakai.

"Yes, we have all heard your story several times, Farmer Mark. I want to hear from John the Human how he came to be in Calimire and wound up in your field."

"Well," John started, pausing briefly to make sure his story was consistent and wouldn't give anything away, "I was in a forest, going for a swim in a little pond, when I found an underwater tunnel. I swam through it and when I came to the surface, found myself here."

"Hmm…that's a very long tunnel. You must be able to hold your breath a very long time for a human."

"Well, I don't like to brag. So you're pretty familiar with humans, then?"

"You are not the first human I have seen. And there is a reason we have not seen more." Malakai paused to indicate a change in topic but started up again before anyone else had a chance to speak. "The king would like to grant you audience. He feels that whenever humans appear in Calimire, it is an omen. I will get the handmaid to provide you with proper attire. A guard will be assigned to you for your protection…and ours. Ask of him any needs you may have." He gestured to the nearest guard. "Please show John the Human to the guest chambers."

***

John's accommodations were quite nice, much to his surprise. He had been expecting more of a dungeon than a suite with a bed (draped in royal purple, of course), a bookcase, and a lovely view of the courtyard. The guard told him to wait there and knock on the door (which was locked from the outside) if he needed anything, for the guard would be positioned outside. The first thing John did was find the chamber pot and make use of it. Never having lived without indoor plumbing, he wasn't quite sure what to do when he was done, and being much too shy to ask the guard, he just slid it back under the bed. "Is that what chambermaids are for?" he thought, trying to remember what he had seen in movies. He tried to imagine what Errol Flynn would do and that brought a faint smile to his face.

He naturally gravitated to the bookshelves. Obviously the authors were all unknown to him, but he did find a book on folktales that got his attention. Lying on his back atop the bed, he delicately cracked the spine and began to read.

The story he read was about a girl who swam in a lagoon and made her way into the land of the humans. There she found loud steel wagons, tall glass buildings, and long, flat rock where there should have been grass. She tried to make her way back home and in the process met three men who offered to help her. The first gave her winged shoes that let her travel quickly. The second gave her a magic compass that always pointed the direction home. And the third gave a magic mirror that would let her see and talk to anyone at any time.

She took these items and began her journey back home. But as she got farther from the city and deeper into the forest, these charms stopped working one by one. And when she sought help, the answer was always the same: you need money to buy a new one. She of course had no money.

Lost and poor, she roamed the sickly yellow streets at night until she stumbled upon the lagoon that had brought her there. It took the last of her strength to make her way back home. And there she was met by family and friends who fed and bathed her and welcomed her back.

The story was called "Chicago."

It wasn't long before he grew tired and fell asleep. And in his slumber, he dreamed.

A little girl in a toy store was walking down the rows past the Barbies and the G.I. Joes and the video games until she found the aisle with the kites.

She took down the one that caught her attention: a vintage kite of wood and plastic. Unlike the ones with the superheroes or cartoons on them, this was simply blue and white.

Taking it from the shelf, she left the store and skipped her way to a nearby park. Finding a clearing, she knelt down and pulled the kite out of its plastic wrapping. This was the first time since the kite was born that it had been in the fresh air.

She positioned the two wooden sticks in a cross form; and it felt so good to the kite to finally feel its wings stretch. It lay on the warm grass, the blades pricking its back and the sun brightly beaming. The kite was getting hot. She tied the string to the cross bar and carefully unspooled it as she slowly walked backward. After a few passes, she pulled the twine taut, turned, and started to run. The kite would lift off a little and then bounce off the grass. It hurt some, but that good kind of pain—too little to really hurt, but just enough to make you feel alive.

And then, then came the time when it soared off into the air, floating. The zephyr wind kept it afloat. When the kite looked down, it saw the little girl smiling and happy. And so too were all the people in the park playing and smiling and happy.

After a while she had her fill and crashed the kite down. She rolled up the twine, broke the cross back into two sticks, and put it back into the plastic sleeve. She brought it home and put it in her closet, never to come out again.

***

He awoke to the sound of knocking on the door. "Visitor!" announced the guard. John arose, quickly tried to straighten his clothes, and made sure his hair was kempt in an effort to look presentable. The queen floated in looking serious and regal: her dress was puffier and she was wearing more jewelry than the night before.

"So you are the human they found in the field?" She was putting on a little show for the benefit of the guard.

"Yes, my lady," he responded, hoping that he was using the proper form of address.

"Here," she whispered as she handed him a vial that had been hidden in one of the folds of her dress.

She resumed her normal speaking voice. "I simply had to see for myself. The king is busy and will not be able to see you until the feast tonight, but my curiosity got the best of me and I could not wait that long. I shall have the princess give you a tour of the castle. I do hope you enjoy your stay." And with that she exited, leaving him with a vial that weighed much, much more than he would have imagined.

***

It wasn't more than a few minutes before the guard announced another visitor: the princess.

"Greetings, John, my name is Julienne. My stepmother asked me to give you a tour of the castle."

"Sounds great…my lady." Again, he had no idea if this was the correct form.

She was slightly taller, slightly thinner, and slightly younger than the queen. Her strawberry-brown hair hung low on her back and shoulders. She held a pleasantly formal tone while trying to keep her attraction hidden. John had a sense of déjà vu.

"Shall we go, then?" she asked.

She started by leading him outside through the courtyard, past the flowers and fountains to the stables. "We have the fastest horses in all the land. My father takes them on hunts when the chance arises."

"Your father must be a very busy man."

"Of course, he is the king after all."

"It must not be easy running a kingdom and keeping everyone happy."

"Well, you cannot expect to keep everyone happy."

"No, I suppose not."

Julienne led John back into the castle and to the dining hall. The table wasn't quite as long as he'd expected. But it was quite clear where the king sat.

"Where do you sit?" John asked Julienne, trying to keep a dialogue going.

"On the right side of the king. I used to sit on the other end by my mother."

"So what happened, if you don't mind me asking?"

"She died not too long ago. I would rather not discuss it. I still miss her dearly." Although he wanted to know much more, he saw she was genuinely upset and dropped the subject. They left the room and headed to the banquet hall in silence.

"As you can see, there is much work being done in preparation for tonight's feast, at which you are to be the guest of honor." There must have been twenty or so people bustling about. Tables were being put up. Dinnerware was being set. Flowers arranged. Musicians were tuning their instruments.

"This is all for me?"

"Well, you are rather special," she said with a smile and a twinkle. He returned the smile tenfold.

The tour ended in the throne room. This too fit the stereotypes for a castle. The throne and the two chairs on either side were set on high, one seat for the queen and the other for the king's advisor. There was, of course, a long red carpet that led to the throne. Julienne explained the layout was meant to intimidate. Those who were to meet the king had to walk down a long path past armed guards and declare their request in front of all—with their necks craned upward, typically on one knee. The large room would make your voice sound small unless you really bellowed.

"What do people typically ask for?"

"It used to mainly be about land: disputes over where cattle could graze or requests for land to farm. But now it has focused on humans. There is a fear the humans are infringing upon our land and destroying our way of life. Some even say we should go to war."

"So that's why all the guards look at me funny. But how many people have actually met a human?"

"Not many. The only one I know for sure is the queen."

"Have you heard of the 'Chicago' fairy tale?"

"The one where the girl meets all the humans?"

"So you have heard of it. Is that the general opinion of humans here?"

"That they take advantage of us? That they treat everything as disposable? That they, in fact, plan obsolescence? They set up false hopes? And they cannot be trusted? That's what the fairy tale is saying and that is what we are told. I can't speak to whether or not that is true. You don't seem that way, at least."

It was then that John recognized her. She was the girl from his first dream, the one who had blown the dust from the sun into the night sky.

On the way back to his room, they passed a long spiral staircase.

"Where does this go?" John asked her.

"Oh, we have a witch that lives here. Her name is Melinda. She has a room to herself at the top of the castle. She doesn't come out much."

"A witch? Really? Why do you have her here?"

"She is very adept at reading signs. Some say she can see the future. My father likes to use what she says to help him make decisions."

"Do you believe in all this?" he asked hesitantly.

"I believe there are omens all around us. Some are just better at seeing them than others."

"Then we should go see her. Ask her about our future."

"Shall we?" She signaled with her hand that he should lead the way. John was a little apprehensive, but refused to let it show. He moved past her, a sly grin on his face.

They stole up the dark, cobwebbed steps, stopping when they reached the top. They looked at the rather large wooden door. They looked at each other. John slowly reached out and knocked, although not too loudly. They waited in silence for a bit. He rapped on the door again, this time a little louder. A dog started barking from somewhere inside the room. They looked at each other again.

"Well?" he asked.

"Let us wait ten seconds and then we will leave."

They waited in silence for a moment.

"Maybe one of us should be counting," she said. They broke out laughing. "Five," she started.

"One," John replied.

"Six."

"Two."

"Ten!" she called and ran down the stairs, giggling the whole time. He followed close behind, chuckling to himself. They ended at the base of the staircase, out of breath more from the laughing than from the running.

She leaned into him, on her tiptoes, hand on his shoulder, and kissed him on the cheek. He couldn't stop smiling.

***

The party began as the sun set. The banquet hall was filled with people and music and laughter. John was a bit intimidated by all the people and looked for a familiar face. He saw the princess and began to relax a little. She made her way toward him.

"Funny seeing you here," she said with a wry smile.

"Yeah, I wasn't sure I could make it but at the last minute figured 'what the heck.'" He tried to keep it going.

"Come, Father wants to see you." She led him by the hand as they snaked through the throng.

The king was surrounded by a group of ten or so people, but the group itself was separate from the rest of the crowd, which was keeping a safe distance out of respect. Or fear. The queen was on his right and Mark was on hers. Upon his seeing them, John's heart raced and his mind was filled with static. He automatically put his hand in his pocket to make sure the vial was still there. His eyes met the queen's, which only made things harder for him.

"Father, this is John," said Julienne.

"Ah, I finally get to meet you. Tell me, what brings you to my land?"

"Well, I was swimming and just happened to end up here."

"Nothing just happens."

There was a brief pause, then one of the king's men ventured to ask, "So what is it like being human?"

"Well, I have no frame of reference—nothing to compare it to. It's all I've ever known," he responded as honestly as he could. They all looked at him askance. All, that is, except Julienne, who nodded in approval.

"Your Highness, the lady Melinda," the high guard announced. In strode a petite girl of fifteen: short and thin with dark green skin, a rougher than most, and black, frazzled, shoulder-length hair. She wore a black dress and had black fingernails. If she wasn't a witch, she at least played the part well. Everyone gave her a wide berth.

"Lady Melinda, I kindly request that you take our guest of honor by the hand and tell us what you see of the worlds beyond, be it good or bad," the king announced as part of some ritual.

John looked nervous as she walked up to him. He held out his right hand and she clasped it within her two much smaller hands. They were clammy and webbed. She slowly closed her eyes for a moment. Inhaled. Exhaled. Then quickly opened her eyes and stared dully at him.

"Soon you will be the next king," she said to John placidly. The crowd lost its breath. John looked at Felicity. She was panicked. Her eyes were wide and her mouth was pursed.

The king looked solemn for a moment. Malakai took over briefly. "Melinda of the Divine, the court thanks you for your talents and bids you good night." The high guards flanked Melinda. She bowed her head slightly (only she could get away with not giving a proper curtsy to the king), turned abruptly, and followed the guards back to her room.

After she was out of sight, the king boomed, "The good lady's premonitions are often filled with enigma. I am still the king—at least for tonight. So let us celebrate!" A moderate cheer rose from the crowd. Despite his attempts at humor, no one believed the king was taking this lightly. Yet everyone followed suit. The band started playing again. Conversations picked up where they had left off. And only in whispers did conversations start on the topic of the new king—and the fall of the old.

King Philip turned to John. "Congratulations," he said jokingly, although John could tell he was forcing it. He clinked his goblet of wine against John's and took a sip. John did the same, watching the king's reaction over the lip of his glass.

"I know, like, how would that even happen?"

“How indeed?” The king put his glass down and continued. “Ah, but either it will happen or it will not. We have no control over fate.”

“That’s one way of looking at things. Removes all responsibility.”

“Does it?”

“Kinda.”

A waiter came by offering bits of cheese to the guests. King Philip put down his glass to take a piece. Felicity took the opportunity to distract the king in conversation. John didn’t really hear what they were talking about; he was too distracted by the looks she kept giving him. These looks shouted: PUT THE POISON IN THE GLASS NOW! He got the message loud and clear, but just stood there with a blank expression. He simply wasn’t going to do it. Period. Exclamation point. After the third attempt, the queen looked to Mark instead. Mark reached into John’s pocket and pulled out the vial. He uncorked it and proceeded to pour an ounce or so into the king’s wineglass. He then handed the vial back to John, who immediately shoved it back into his pocket.

Felicity excused herself. Mark raised his glass in a toast to “The old king and the new,” and smiled broadly, eyes arcing from the king to John as he spoke. The king did not seem too happy about the toast but still took a gulp and put the glass back down. Then it all hit John at once. He was never going to be king, he was just a patsy. Someone to take the fall while Felicity married Mark. His heart sank, his stomach knotted and the rest of him felt numb.

John wasn’t sure how long the poison would take. Minutes passed in gut-wrenching anxiety until finally the king said he was not feeling well and immediately collapsed. The crowd gasped and the guards rushed over to extract the king at once.

***

John sat in his cell, head down, forearms on knees. "This isn't as nice as the guest room," he thought. The cold stone walls and smells of mold and urine supported his opinion. Things seemed rather hopeless.

The king had been murdered.

He had been imprisoned and sentenced to death by the queen.

Felicity and Mark were engaged to be married in a week; which would of course make Mark king.

So it looked as if Melinda's prophecy would not come true after all. Not only would John not be king, he would not even be alive.

Hopeless indeed.

The cell door opened. Julienne entered with a guard close behind. She turned to the sentry and gave him a slight nod. He left, closing the heavy door behind him. She waited to hear it shut before she began to speak.

"I do not understand. I would not have taken you for a killer, John."

"I'm not. I was framed—by Felicity and Mark."

"But you had a vial of poison on you."

John proceeded to explain what had happened. It took a little time but Julienne ended up believing him, mostly because she believed in him.

"Things are not well for me either. I loved my father, John. Now he is gone forever and I never had the chance to say good-bye, to say that I cared, to tell him how much he meant. I have become alone, orphaned. Felicity never cared for me. And now that my father is not here to protect me, I fear that she will have me exiled. Or worse. Sad, sad days." She stared into his eyes. "Oh, John!" she breathed as she leaned into him with a powerful hug. Her voice trembled and her eyes watered gently. John swallowed his tears. The words "I love you" escaped from his mouth in a whisper only for her ears. It was ridiculous. He barely knew her. She recoiled and held him at arm's length, studying his face for sincerity. She began to cry. Unable to return his feelings in words, she gently held his face in her hands, smiled broadly, and softly nodded. She knew how ridiculous it was too, and could not bring herself to speak those same words. But there was something magical in the moment. They sat and held each other for a while in a calmness steeped in gleeful absurdity.

"You know, if we were to marry, you would be king."

"Really?" John replied, surprised by both parts of that sentence.

"Yes. I have royal blood in my veins. She does not."

"It seems like that would solve everything." He got down on one knee. "Julienne, will you marry me?" John was amused that in the span of two days, he had turned into a rash person. Again, he wasn't sure if that was a good thing or a bad thing.

***

Things happened very quickly. Julienne ordered the guard to summon Malakai. She explained their plan quickly to the grand inquisitor, who, of course, had questions.

"By law and custom, you are correct; you would be the next king and queen. And I too am uncomfortable with Felicity ruling the kingdom through Mark. For she wants war, and that is good for no one. But John is a human, and untrustworthy by nature. We do not know enough to prove otherwise. Everything he has said so far could be a lie."

"You know as well as I do, Malakai, trust is earned over time—something we have little of. What else can we do?" asked Julienne.

Malakai thought for a moment, staring hard at the floor. His face lightened when the idea came to him. He first made eye contact with Julienne and then with John. "Answer me this, John, and if I find it satisfactory, I shall call the priest myself."

John imagined he was Batman and Malakai was the Riddler from that sixties TV show. He felt the urge to break into a Batusi. His hips started to sway ever so slightly; his fingers twitched into V's. "Snap out of it," he chided himself.

"Say you are king, and a man steals a horse from your stable. How do you respond?"

"That's not a riddle," John thought, slightly disappointed. Then he quickly responded, "I give him a saddle."

Malakai was more than a little surprised by that response. "Why is that?"

"He needs it more than I do. And he will feel indebted to me. Those with true power rarely need to actually exercise it."

"Interesting. I must say, I have never heard that response before. There is hope for you." Malakai glanced at Julienne, who was smiling broadly. He shouted to the guard, "Send for the high priest at once!"

***

The marriage took place right there in the cell within a matter of minutes. They had to move quickly to keep it a secret from Felicity. The couple said their vows, interspersing them with genuine, yet awkward, smiles. When the rite was complete, Malakai called Felicity, Mark, Julienne, and John to the royal court.

"What is this about?" asked Felicity, a little indignant.

"It is time to have the official proclamation ceremony for the next king and queen," said Malakai.

"That may be fine, but why is John here and not in his cell?"

"Why, he is the next king," replied Malakai.

"We are married and your rule is over before it even began," added Julienne.

"What! No!" Felicity was incredulous, enraged, defiant. "Guards, take them both to the dungeon!" No one moved.

"Guards, take them to a cell," ordered Malakai.

The guards moved in. There was no real struggle. Felicity and Mark left with little ado, but there was fire in their eyes. Flames flared at John and Julienne as they walked past. Malakai proceeded with the private, official ceremony. John and Julienne were both a bit dazed by the whole experience and sleepwalked through the ritual.

The next day an announcement was made to the kingdom, and a week after that was the celebration in which the new king and queen were presented to their subjects. Some people were indifferent, but most were skeptical of a human king (to put it nicely).

John's first act as king was to expel Felicity and Mark and the rest of Felicity's lovers from the kingdom (for fear of any uprising or backlash). Julienne and John proved to be a dynamic duo, as John said—a joke that only he got. Julienne educated John on the customs and sensibilities of her people. John brought his experiences as a human to bear. And although they didn't make all the right decisions, they always had the people's best interests in mind. The kingdom prospered. The people rejoiced.

Soon enough, John and Julienne had a child—a girl. She was smart and pretty. And when she was old enough they read fairy tales to her. She especially liked the one where the princess met a brave knight from a faraway land who saved her from the evil stepmother. They married, ruled the kingdom justly, and lived happily ever after.

My All

And with that, she set out to seek her fortune. She made her way through the woods, and it wasn't long before she came upon a robin near death. "Dear girl, have pity on me, for I am about to die and I don't want to leave a bloody corpse." She took the bird to a nearby stream, where she cleaned its wounds. And as the blood mixed with the water, it collected on the riverbed and formed rubies, which she then collected. "Dear bird, you dropped these rubies," she said. The bird choked out, "Alas, I have no use for them anymore. Please keep them as a token of my gratitude." She thanked the bird and bid him farewell.

Farther down the trail, she saw a mauled sable that called out, "Dear girl, have pity on me, for I am about to die and I don't want to leave unkempt remains." So she brushed the fur of the frail beast, and with each stroke, diamonds fell out. She gathered the diamonds and presented them to the sable. "Dear sable, I believe these are yours." The sable replied, "Keep them as a reward for a job well done." She thanked him kindly and moved on.

Then she came upon a clearing, the center of which held a tree unlike any she had seen before. The branches were many and thin and they sprouted from the thick trunk, giving the tree the shape of a large mushroom.

Under the tree, resting against the trunk, lay a man. But no ordinary man was he, for he lacked any features upon his face.

She took pity on the man who lay motionless, and thought to use the gems to help him. So she knelt next to the man, and gently set the rubies where his eyes would go. Immediately they attached themselves and eyelids grew. Slowly they blinked. He squinted to focus and looked at her. Then she put the diamonds where his teeth would be. Lips formed and parted. A smile crossed his face. Eyes glowing, teeth sparkling, he came to life.

"Dear girl, you saved me."

"From what, dear sir?"

"My girl, from a life of death."

"And how did this come about, my liege?"

"My love, I was cursed by the witch who owns this forest."

"But why, my lord?"

"My one, for what happened to her children."

"And what was that?"

"This, my all." And with that he ate her.

Hunger Pangs

Man, was I hungry. There was nothing to eat in the house so I ordered a large pizza and ate the whole thing—but I was *still* starving. So I searched for something, anything, to eat. Couldn't find a thing. Not a slice of bread. Not a cracker. Not even a crumb. I scoured the cupboards, the fridge, the seat cushions, the floor, behind the stove—nothin'.

I had to look elsewhere.

That's when I ate my pride. It was too hard to bite or chew, so I swallowed it whole. Nearly choked on the damn thing, but I managed to get it down. It wasn't enough, though. I wanted…no, I *needed* more.

So I boiled my hate. Each mouthful more bitter than the last. My stomach growled for more.

I whipped up a bowl of pity. Creamy and sweet, it went down easy.

Love? There hasn't been any of *that* around here for a long time. No…I stopped looking for love. Instead I drank my tears and belched my apologies.

Then I found a bit of hope. Stale and moldy as it was, I took a bite. That was a mistake. I couldn't keep it down. Just made room for more.

Confidence was a tasty morsel: meaty and juicy. What do they call it? Savory? Yeah, savory.

That was it. There was nothing left. I've eaten it all and it's left me so fuckin' big I can't get out of bed. But that's OK; I don't need to go anywhere. I'm not hungry…for now.

Tomorrow it starts all over again.

Applebite

--- The Forest: Where All Things Begin ---

Maggie stumbled through the forest. Her left hand held an apple. The other grasped a knife. A large, heavy knife that hung low and caused her to limp. So shiny new was this blade that it appeared to glow in the predawn haze. The early morning air was still clammy and cool and thick. Her breaths were shallow, stifled.

She couldn't sleep. But this was nothing new. Restful sleep was rare of late due to the dreams. Although she couldn't really recall much about them, she woke every few minutes with a sense of dread. A sense that something was forgotten. Or lost. She had begun to make a habit of walking to this nearby forest to clear her head. During the day, Maggie found it to be tranquil and calming. But at night it was different. She brought a knife for protection, for who knows what dangers awaited in this dreary forest.

She was in her thirties, though you wouldn't have guessed it. On good days she could be mistaken for a teenager (much to her delight). At times, that might have had more to do with how she dressed than her youthful complexion. She had never entirely outgrown her Goth/punk look, although over the years the hard edge might have receded a little. But she still wore a lot of black, some flowing vintage dresses and the ever-present Doc Martens. Her dark hair swooped several inches below her shoulders, sharply framing her ashen face. She was thin but more the wiry kind of thin than the frail kind.

And now, with the sun rising, that sleepy underwater feeling began to fade with the morning mist, only to be replaced with utter boredom. With each step, she swung the blade haphazardly as if hoping to strike something. As Maggie hobbled along, she took a large bite of the apple. Finding it past its prime, mealy and starchy sweet, she tossed it aside. She happened across a mossy log weathered and crumbling and set herself down upon it. She stared glassy-eyed at nothing in particular as she absentmindedly stabbed the tree trunk over and over. Behind her, the apple she had abandoned drew the attention of the nearby crows. They quickly lit on it and began to peck violently, leaving tiny cuts and nicks. But then something uncanny happened. It wasn't obvious at first—it as the birds were aggressively feeding on it—but soon it became clear; the apple was moving on its own.

It started to shake and grow very fast. The birds became scared. They flopped and sputtered and flew away in harried retreat. Maggie took notice of the squawking commotion behind her and casually looked over her shoulder to see, much to her surprise, a fully grown tree—of a kind she had never seen before. Of a kind no one had seen before.

She sauntered over, her grip on the knife steady. Hanging from the tree were cocoons, large ones that drooped like some kind of obscene fruit. The shell of each cocoon looked like artichoke leaves that had been welded together. Maggie grabbed the bottom tip of the nearest one with her left hand and pulled it down so it was just below eye level. She raised the knife slowly, the sharp blade jutting down from the heel of her hand, and stabbed deeply into the bulging cocoon.

It bled.

Red drops puddled slowly at her feet. The puddle grew as more and more drops fell. And more still, until it was raining blood. Maggie pulled down the knife that was still lodged in the sac, and slit the fleshy casing wide open. She spread the sides apart to reveal a child, a tiny humanoid baby. She drew her blade again, slicing swiftly and harshly, cutting the umbilical cord and freeing the child from the tree. She laid the child on the ground and rapidly got to work cutting down all the other cocoons. Each one she tossed into a pile that quickly grew. The crows that were still on the periphery, still waiting, still hungry, decided to investigate and started picking at the husks. Bits were taken out of flesh and foliage. Maggie shooed them away, waving her arms wildly to make herself seem big. She accidentally made contact with one of the birds, striking it down with her blade. It tumbled from the air, crashed hard, and rolled on the forest floor. She watched it come to a rest, yet it still appeared to be moving. Well, not really moving, but pulsing. A red glow hummed from the bird. She edged closer. It was the eye. The left eye glowed a soft red. Maggie used her knife to pluck the strobing orb out and threw it on top of the pile of cocoons. She raised her arms and from the ground sprung a rickety wooden fence. It surrounded the tree and the cocoons and her. Maggie beheld this makeshift cemetery she had created. The birds would now keep their distance, she knew. Maggie turned to leave for home, knife in one hand while the other held the child upside down, by the ankle.

~~~ *Of Dreams*

As a child, Maggie had vivid dreams. Most would vaporize in the light of the morning sun, but others sat heavy in her memory. Those few that remained with her had something in common. They all centered around flight.

Several of these dreams were very similar. They intermixed frustration and joy. You see, even though she had the gift of flight, it wasn't the kind of boundless wonder you see in movies or comics; it was a struggle. She could barely get off the ground, maybe a foot or two before awkwardly collapsing back to earth. These forays were little better than the slow-motion hops you would see astronauts taking on the moon. Similar dreams had her fly for much longer periods and be in full control, yet she could get only inches off the ground. No one would even notice that she was flying, and she was much too shy to point it out to anyone for fear of being ridiculed for bragging. Still, she knew this gift was rare. She knew it was special.

Other dreams had her in the middle of a highway, cars speeding toward her. She was taller, heavier than normal. She would spread her arms out and see that they were no longer arms, but in fact blackly feathered wings. In broad inky strokes, she would slowly flap. These strokes generated powerful winds that would slow the cars down, forcing some off the road while flipping others over.

And on this cold winter's night, six-year-old Maggie dreamt. She was lying on her back in a grassy field. Her hands were folded behind her head. The sun shone down warmly. She saw a black dot in the sky right above her. It was falling, and as it grew closer it began to stretch into a thin line. Soon she recognized it—a black feather gently twirling down toward her. She stared at it lazily, letting it hypnotize her. When it finally landed no more than two feet away, she sat up and saw more feathers falling from the sky before her. They formed a trail with the farther ones higher in the sky, ascending like a staircase. They were spaced perfectly, about a hundred meters apart, so that in the time it took to walk to the next one, the feather had fallen close enough to her that she could reach up and pluck it out of the air. She followed these feathers, skipping over hills and dales, slogging through rivers and tiptoeing over bridges, until she came to a waterfall. She scaled the steep craggy hill to reach the top, whereupon she saw a murky figure in the distance. Immediately she knew there was something wrong. Her stomach seized up. Her breath turned into short staccato gasps. She approached from its blind side as it gazed into the distance. But it wasn't a man, not really. It stood like a man, on two legs. But it was some sort of hybrid, some type of chimera. The head was that of a raven. Feathers swept down the torso, leading to large wings that were folded at its sides and covered most of the back. But the rest was a male human form. Afraid to get too close, afraid to be heard or seen, she stopped a good hundred yards away. It didn't matter. The creature slowly turned its head toward her. Her heart raced. She woke up in tears.

--- Home ---

Her home was dreary. The outside was a simple affair, almost to the point of being crude. The few windows that dotted the home were small and tucked away on upper floors. Inside it was dark and dank. The kind of darkness that made you feel blind when you entered. And when you left, you felt as if you were being stabbed with knives made out of light. The house was run-down, the furniture old. It all was functional, mind you, but you wouldn’t want to sit on it, or touch it for that matter. Candles provided most of the light.

Maggie, hands full, kicked open the front door. It was never locked; no one would bother robbing it and most people were too wary to venture close due to rumors of hoarding/meth lab/witchcraft. Her posture was slightly hunched, unusual for someone so young, but her strides were quick and purposeful. She had been living here since she was a child, the last ten years or so by herself. Flies buzzed about here and there. The home wasn’t particularly dirty, nor particularly clean, it was just that time of year when pests choked the air. And windows without screens didn’t really help. She blithely swiped with her knife at one that got too close.

Thump.

She dropped the baby on the large wooden dining table. It landed on its bottom and wobbled from side to side, but managed to stay upright.

“Are you my mother?” the child asked.

Maggie stopped dead in her tracks and stared at it warily. Slowly she pulled back the chair next to her, never taking her eyes off the infant. She noticed it had grown in the time it took to walk home and was no longer a newborn, but a infant of around six months. Having made a mental note to calculate its rate of growth later, she sat down, landing almost at eye level with the child. They stared silently for a moment, Maggie’ s expression serious, the child’ s blank, calm, almost happy. She paused before responding.

“No. Never call me Mother.” She stressed this part, then continued. “And what form of creature are you?”

“I don’ t know, I’ m just born.”

“Right.”

“I’ m hungry.”

“What do you want to eat?” The initial shock subsiding, Maggie decided to just go with it.

“Food.”

“Ugh. OK, well, I used to have an apple somewhere.”

“No!” and the boy started to cry.

“What do you eat, then?”

“Doggie!”

“How about some milk?”

“Yay!”

She got a bowl out of the cupboard and milk out of the fridge. She laid the bowl in front of the child and it greedily lapped up the milk.

“Look. I have to go to work. Will you be OK on your own?”

“Yes.”

--- Away ---

Maggie left the house, umbrella tucked under her arm (the full kind with the curved handle that can be used as a walking stick—not the mini folding kind that has no sense of grace). She was a firm believer that it rains only if you are unprepared. The sky rumbled its dissent.

She strolled down the backwoods shortcut she always took to work. Trees littered with crows crowded the dirt path. They seemed to be watching her; their caws to be directed at her. The rain started to fall, gently, somewhat pleasantly. If she had been heading home she would have let it wash over her, but sitting in wet clothes all day was not appealing. She tugged the umbrella open, perching the black canopy over her. She held it rigidly, making sure it stood tall and proper.

The trees were now thick with black birds. Their caws seemed to increase in frequency and intensity with the rain. It sounded as if they were calling out her name:

Mag-*gie* Mag-*gie*

One was so bold as to fly down to the middle of the path in front of her. It flapped its wings a few times and shifted its weight between its talons before settling down. Maggie stopped to take this in; the patter of rain splashing off her umbrella peppered her ears, mixing with the din of the crows. Then the crow spoke.

“The child is not yours. Not your flesh. Nor your bone. Return it. Give it back. To our God.” Its voice cracked and screeched.

“God and I are not on speaking terms. So no. I will watch over the child myself, thanks.”

“Our God is powerful. Watching from above. Ever present. His judgment is final. His vengeance is swift. Return the child now. To the field. Where he was found. You will not be asked again.”

The crows were all silent. Watching for her response.

She ran.

Back toward the child, toward home. The birds took to the air en masse, flapping and screeching. Some flew at her and some flew toward her house, but one, the messenger, flew in the opposite direction, toward the cold north. Toward its master.

Maggie jettisoned the umbrella to the side. The wind and rain caught it and swooped it up into the air. Its ribs elongated, the black webbing stretched. It morphed and grew to life. Moving like some devil squid, it gulped legions of birds in one swoop, then spat them to the ground covered in some transparent goo that made their wings useless. It repeated, sweeping left and then right, but there were too many of them. Maggie kept running home. She shot through the front door and slammed it behind her.

The child sat on the table, where he was in the middle of building a miniature city out of toothpicks and sugar cubes. Maggie rushed over, snatched him up with both arms, and fled to the bathroom. Birds crashed through the windows and flung themselves at the bathroom door. The scratching and thumping and pecking went on for hours. Maggie was on edge, but hid it fairly well. The boy seemed unaffected, happy to splash in the tub until he was tired enough to nap. Eventually things slowed down and the last crow fluttered away tired and demoralized.

She knew they couldn't stay. That this respite would be short. God was coming for her child.

~~~ *Prayers Answered*

"Maggie, brush your teeth, say your prayers, and go to bed."

"But Mom!" Maggie whined.

"Now!"

Maggie dragged her slipper-shod feet to the bathroom, in some sort of jumbled impersonation of Frankenstein's monster and a teenager. But once she squeezed a gooey mess of paste onto her toothbrush, her mood lightened. Brushing vigorously, she made as much foam as she could. She imagined herself a rabid dog. Made a white beard. Drooled into the sink. Added more toothpaste and started over.

"Maggie, you've been in there for twenty minutes! Bed! Now!" her mother called from somewhere, probably darning socks in front of the TV. Maggie rinsed and wiped her face with the ever-damp hand towel, getting some of the mess off before heading to her bedroom.

She knelt down on the hard, creaky wooden floors of her room, and propped her elbows on her bed. Clasping her hands tightly, she shut her eyes and bowed her head until it touched her knuckles. She never quite knew what to make of prayer. There was a sense of excitement, the ability to talk to God and share thoughts or secrets or ask for things. Or even just talk. But the one-way conversations made her feel awkward at times. Maybe God was too busy with more important prayers. Maybe she needed to be more interesting. On nights when she got self-conscious, she would default to the old standbys: the pre-formulated prayers taught in school that standardized and impersonalized everything.

Tonight was not one of those nights.

"Dear God. Today was a good day. We went to the store and I got some candy. I played hide-and-seek with Mommy. Daddy isn't home yet. Can you say hi to him for me?

"Sometimes I get lonely. I don't tell anyone else about it. They worry that I'm sad all the time. I'm worried that Mommy and Daddy might die. Like Jamie did."

"I will always be there for you," a voice from everywhere and nowhere answered.

"God?"

"Yes, Maggie."

"Why did Jamie die?"

"Because I need him here, with me."

"But I need him too."

"I know it hurts. But I also know that you are strong. You don't know how strong yet. I know you can handle it or I would not give you this responsibility. Can you be strong for me?"

"Yes. I love you, God."

"I love you, child."

"Amen."

--- Aztok ex machina ---

It was a warm, sunny day. The cloudless blue sky cheered her spirits. Maggie walked through the ankle-high grass with the child in tow. She didn't have a clear destination. Maybe head toward the city—seek asylum there. She put her thoughts on hold when a shadow passed over the two them. Looking up, she saw a huge black bird flying overhead. It circled and landed just ahead of them. Easily twenty feet tall, it towered over the two travelers.

"Give me the child."

"No."

"It is not one of your kind. Give it to me and I will take care of it."

"No."

"It is more powerful than you know. It is beyond your understanding. It is evil and it will consume you."

"I can take care of myself. I've been doing it for a while now."

"Then I shall take it. By force. I will crush its bones with my beak. Its blood shall drip down my throat."

Maggie clutched the child tight. "Screw you, Aztok." The bird straightened its back and flapped its wings at her, generating a punishing wind. Smaller trees bent over, the tops nearly touching the ground. Larger ones creaked while branches blew off. The grass danced in waves. Maggie fell forward to the ground, on top of the child, protecting it. The black bird took to the air. It buzzed just over her before turning skyward. It rose high, then looped and dove at them. She rose to her knees, still holding the child. As Aztok approached, she steeled herself until the last moment, when the talons were within feet, and then she rolled to the right, out of harm's way. The bird zoomed several hundred feet behind her. She ran. Ran for the forest. They both knew Aztok could not track them in among the tall trees. She ran with all her might. The child weighed her down considerably. Her legs were heavy. Her heart thumped. Her lungs were afire. Her vision blurred. She could hear the beating of the wings grow louder. And she kept running. Luckily, she didn't have to make it all the way into the woods, just close enough. The bird veered skyward before it could reach them, avoiding the edge of the forest.

She kept moving for a bit, trudging slowly among the pines and birches. She would look skyward from time to time and see Aztok circling overhead. Waiting. Weariness overwhelmed Maggie and she eventually collapsed. The child looked up at her as she leaned back against a tree, her head tilted skyward, eyes closed.

"Why me?"

"You need a name."

"My name is Max."

"I see," said Maggie, always amused by the child. "How did you pick that?"

"You're stalling."

"Well, *Max*, Aztok is afraid of you. He is afraid you will take his place. He's afraid that you will become the next god and he will be no more. He wants you so he can destroy you. But I won't let that happen."

"But I mean, why me in the first place? Back when you plucked me from the tree, you spared me, but you destroyed all my brothers and sisters."

"You can remember that? I guess I shouldn't be surprised. I knew there was something special about that tree. And the fruit that grew there. I knew you were a part of me and a part of something powerful. The others were too, but not as strong. And there were too many of them, I couldn't have cared for you all. And Aztok would want to destroy all of you anyway. Maybe I was hoping he wouldn't notice one was missing. He claims everything is his, that he created it all. He's right in that you are one of his kind and that you're powerful. At some point, you may be able to take his place, but not now. You're not ready yet."

“Am I really evil?”

“No more so than anyone else.”

“Including god?”

“Especially god.”

~~~ *Like Father*

“Where do your allegiances lie?” It was an interesting question. One that you don’t really expect to come from your father, especially when you are eleven. It had been dark for hours now and Maggie was getting tired.

“It just feels wrong,” Maggie said quietly.

“I’m your father. I say what’s right and what’s wrong. You better start worrying about what will happen if you don’t do like I told you, instead of what ‘feels’ right.” He stared her down. “Now you want to be a good girl, don’t you?”

“Yes.”

“You want to make your father proud?”

“Yes.”

“Then do what I ask and don’t tell your mother about this. She would just worry.”

Maggie picked up the shovel and got to work. In her head, she whispered her prayers. “Give me the wisdom, Lord, to know right from wrong. And the strength to follow through,” she thought. “I could really use some guidance.

I know I'm supposed to respect my father. And he probably has a good reason for this, but I can't see it." She waited for a response. Then finally, "Is your silence the answer? Just as I should trust in your plan for me, so too I should trust in my father's?"

Her body relaxed and she began to dig faster.

--- Arcstone ---

They trudged through the forest's uneven land. Vines grew everywhere, reaching skyward like tiny hands from the grave trying to trip them up. Trying to keep them here. Ahead, a teenage boy sat very still, eyes wide, looking a little scared. As if he were hoping not to be noticed.

"Hi," Max called out as he waved to the teen. At this point, after only a few days, he had the appearance of an eight-year-old.

"Um…hello?" replied the teen, seeming a little dismayed that he had been spotted so easily.

"What's your name?"

"David."

"Hello, David, I'm Max. What are you doing here by yourself?"

"Uh, I'm on my way to the Church of Life to offer my Arcstone."

A surprisingly large cube-shaped stone lay next to him. Roughly the size of a large pumpkin, it must have weighed at least thirty pounds. There were chips and notches taken out of it and a hole in the middle about an inch in diameter that seemed to go straight down through to the other side. David rested his hand on it to indicate that this was the stone he was talking about—although it was pretty apparent. It sat next to him like a dull, chunky friend. He looked at both of them sheepishly—as if expecting mockery but secretly hoping for a compliment.

"That's far. It will take you days to get there on foot," Maggie said with a hint of concern.

"Well, I've already been traveling for a couple of months now."

"You've been lugging that stone the whole time?" Max asked incredulously.

"He's a Lifer," Maggie said. "Every Lifer must take their Arcstone to the church, where it is added to all the others. Their cathedral is built out of these stones."

"Yeah. I haven't seen it, but I hear it's amazing—it's huge and it grows every day. This stone will join my parents' and their parents' and so on, going back centuries." It was clear to Maggie that David was a gentle soul. His inner childlike enthusiasm and kindness were cloaked by his shyness, which seemed to manifest in a social awkwardness that made it difficult for him to connect with others. He wouldn't make eye contact and rarely looked in their direction, preferring to look at the stone or his feet. At times he whispered or stuttered slightly. But she could tell that he was very proud of his stone and his journey. She knew that if he kept on this topic, he would open up a little and his enthusiasm would get the better of him. She also knew Max's curiosity would help.

Max asked, "When will it be finished?"

"Probably never. When one part is complete, they add a new annex or wing or something."

"So how does it work? Do you just go there and put your stone wherever you want?"

"Well, it's…it's really more of a ritual. So when I present my stone, there will be a ceremony, and I will become a member of the church. The Arcstone holds my story—each one is different."

"How come I don't have an Arcstone?" Max asked Maggie.

"Because we are not Lifers."

"Well, I want one. How did you get yours?" he asked David. "From a quarry?"

"OK, well, mine, like everyone else's, was given to me at birth. My mom and dad selected it based on where and when I was born. The stone is feldspar. It symbolizes strength, durability, and um, you know, utility. People under this stone are reliable and good contributors to the town. It is often used for making glass and pottery."

"How come yours has all these scars on it?" David smiled at Max's use of the word *scars*.

"You're supposed to have markings on it, to shape it, to make it your own. Those 'scars' tell the story of it. They give it character." David moved the rock to his lap so he could point out the markings as he spoke. "See, this chip came from the first time I tried to lift it. I was three and it was too heavy, but somehow I managed to get it off the floor and immediately dropped it. It left a chip in the stone and a crack in the tile floor. And this scratch, it came from my brother. We were fooling around and he got angry and kicked it down the stairs. When my dad found out, he got on my brother pretty good. And this brown spot here, this came in the first week of my journey. I was walking down to a small river to get some water. The bank was like really steep and I slipped and it fell from my hands and smacked against a tree. I cut myself on some sharp rocks while trying to break my fall. Like an idiot, I went to go pick up my stone before washing my hands off in the river and got blood all over it. I was able to clean most of it off, but you can still see a little of it."

"That's so cool. I *need* to see this—the temple, the stones, the ceremony," Max said to Maggie. Then, turning to David, "Can we join you?"

"Uh, yeah. I mean, it would be nice to have some company."

"Mom, can we?" Max pleaded.

"Don't call me Mom. Yes, we can, but David, I should warn you, you're actually adding *three* to your party. Max, me, and the devil himself."

~~~ ***Still***
~~~

Her mother was getting worse. The miscarriages had an effect on her—physically and mentally. They poisoned her. She had seen only one doctor over the years, when they took her to the ER because the bleeding wouldn't stop. Her father felt doctors interfered with God's plan. Her mother felt this way too, at least she had before she got sick. Now that Maggie was a little older, just entering her teens, she started to have her own views on this. Maggie thought this aversion to modern medicine was about more than just religion. She felt money played a role here too. Although they weren't destitute, money was always an issue. Maybe some payments were late. Maybe there were some days the electricity was shut off, yet it always got turned back on again. But doctor's bills, those were an extravagance. God would provide, her father asserted. Sickness was a sign of a weak constitution, a bad soul. The Lord would heal the good and righteous.

The pain and depression changed her mother over time. They stripped away the veneer of warmth and warped her core. She had no patience to be nice. She slept often and when she was awake she cursed at the pain and anyone nearby. Maggie knew deep down her mother still loved her, and she still loved her mother, but her mother just wasn't herself anymore.

One night, while her father was out avoiding his life, Maggie hid in her room and did the only thing she could.

"God, please don't take my mom. I'm afraid. My family is quickly falling apart. Dad is hardly ever here, and if Mom is gone, he may never come back.

"I'm sorry. I'm sorry for all the times I got frustrated with my mother. I'm sorry for every swear word I uttered under my breath. I've confessed my sins, and I'll do my penance. We are not bad people, Lord, but we are weak. I will try to be a better person. I will praise You daily. I will treat others with respect and kindness. Please, just make my mom better." She closed her eyes as they began to bead with tears, and in the blackness she saw their church. The lights flickered inside. The windows glowed.

She put on her boots and sneaked out the back door. Her mother was asleep, but the pain had kept it from being a peaceful sleep and she would wake at the softest of sounds. Maggie hiked through the backyards and down the narrow lanes of this small town. Soon enough the aged white building appeared. A weathered bronze bell hung still in the steeple. Two black birds sat on the roof like sentries guarding a tiny castle. When she got close enough, they cawed as if saying, "Halt. Who goes there?"

The lights were on. The door was unlocked. She crept in.

A dove sat in the middle of the large round stained glass window. It eyed her for a second before it flew down to the altar.

It spoke. "Know that you are loved, Margaret. I have shown it in so many ways. So many times. I have provided for you when you needed it. I have given you food and light and warmth. Earth and sky. I have given you life. But not without cost. Everything I give, every life I create, weakens me. I used to be the universe, and now I am but a dove.

“And still you ask for more.

“My life is yours. But so too is your life mine. I will not let harm come to you, just as you will not let harm come to me.”

Maggie was confused and ashamed. She could feel her face flush. She wanted to disappear.

“I’m sorry. I’ll leave.”

“Go home, Maggie. Back to your mother. Make your peace with her.”

Maggie turned and left. She swallowed hard to choke down her emotions until they plunged like a stone into her belly, weighing her down. Making her logy and nauseous.

She headed back home, each step feeling heavier than the last, as if she were sinking, yet she couldn’t stop running. All the while her tears flowed steadily.

She arrived home to silence. She held her side, slightly bent over from cramps, still breathing heavily. She pulled off her boots and tiptoed to her parents’ bedroom. It was dark, and at first all she could see was a shadowy figure rustling on the bed. She gasped as her eyes adjusted, realizing that the shadow was not her mother, but a murder of crows pulling and tearing bits of flesh from her mother’s carcass. They covered every inch of her, feeding ravenously, oblivious to Maggie’s presence.

Maggie screamed as loud and as long as she could until she voided her lungs of any air. She passed out. Her father woke her hours later.

"Oh my God, Dad, did you see the birds? Did you catch any of them?" Maggie's speech was confused, sleepy, almost childlike.

"What birds?" Her father spoke in his most soothing voice as he gently brushed her hair. His wife's death transporting him back in time.

"On the bed, they were eating her." But there were no birds nor signs of their feeding. Only her mother lying in bed, eerily still.

The funeral was large but subdued. Family flocked in from miles around to pay respects. Several aunts took turns staying at their home for weeks at a time, cooking and cleaning. Maggie was appreciative but could not show it. Her anger always tainted her interactions. It showed up as brooding silence, or childish impudence, or typical teenage rebellion. They took it in stride and sympathized as best they could. The nicer they were, the meaner she was. It fed upon itself. Each new day, the Rubicon got further and further behind her.

Her father got the worst of it. Her aunts and grandmothers were just in the way. But her father, well, he deserved her anger. He had let her mother—his wife, whom he supposedly loved—die. And even though he seemed to remember that he was a father, and had responsibilities, it didn't matter. He was more dead to her than her mother. But as much as she lashed out at him, she knew this too was misdirected. He never really could have saved her mother. He was just as powerless as she was. Oh, he wasn't innocent. He had his faults. But there was one who could have really done something. One who was really to blame.

--- Machine Man ---

The summer air was sticky sweet. The occasional breeze kept it from being stifling. It made Maggie want to stop right there and grow roots. They had been walking for an hour or so through the waist-high straw. Max tagged along methodically, dutifully, without a single complaint. David took the rear, lugging his stone and smiling the whole time. Maggie led by a step. Her vigilance nearly hid how tired she was.

They soon came to a clear patch—a rectangle a couple of acres long where the wheat had been cut clean. A man was bundling the shafts by hand. Wearing a typical farmer's outfit—straw hat, overalls, gloves—he seemed a bit stiff in his movements—arthritic almost. Maggie guessed he was in his mid forties. He appeared very much in the moment, simply focusing on the task at hand, not rushing through or lollygagging as others might do for these types of tasks. His warm, craggy face had a slight smile on it. He seemed nice enough to Maggie that she approached him.

"Excuse me." Maggie spoke louder than usual to get his attention, but also from the unjustified assumption that he was hard of hearing.

"Yes?"

"Do you mind if we cut through your farm? The travel will be much easier."

"It's not my farm. It's my creator's."

"Creator's?"

"Mr. Johnson owns this farm."

"And he *created* you?"

"Yes, I am an android."

"Really? I didn't know such things existed."

"I am the only one I am aware of."

"Well, can we ask your creator then?"

"No."

"Why not?"

"He died several years ago."

"Well, how about his wife or whoever runs the farm now?"

"His wife died the year he created me. They had no children. In fact, there are no humans on this land."

"Then who are you doing all this for?" She pointed to the bales of hay.

"No one."

"So why do you do it?"

“It is what I was created to do. I also cook, clean, sew, and perform well over a thousand other functions.”

Max followed intently, not saying a word. His head bobbing back and forth.

“Could we stay at the house tonight? Would there be food to share?”

“Yes. Follow me.”

The home lived in conflict with itself. The rustic, worn wood structure supported innumerable gadgets and gizmos, cogs and chips and tools from crowbars to electron microscopes. The lab was a mad scientist’s dream, an homage to technology. The part that was a home, the kitchen, living room, bedroom, was clean and structured—a well-maintained museum. But there were a few touches of home. Maggie found a picture of the farmer and his wife.

“You look just like him,” she said to the bot. “Why were you made humanoid? I wouldn’t think that would be the most efficient way to farm. I mean, why not a tractor?”

“People relate to things that look like them.”

“Tell me again, why do you keep working on the farm?” Max asked.

“That’s what I was built to do.”

“But there is no point.”

“I have no need for the end result, true. I cannot eat wheat. I do not need it to sustain myself and I have no use for any money that could be made from selling it. However, it is not about the results. It is about doing."

"But why do this? You could do anything you want."

"I don't have wants. I only have needs."

"So if you had no farm, or if the crops didn't grow, what would you do?"

"Nothing."

The boy smiled. "You're coming with us. Mom, can we take him with?"

Maggie ignored the "Mom" reference. "I don't think it would be appropriate."

"This is my home. I need to stay here and tend to it."

"But I really want him!"

"He is not your toy, Max. He is not a plaything. And he is not coming with."

"But…"

"That's final."

They started their journey the next morning, early. The sky was painted yellow and blue but the sun hadn't started to crown yet. Grasshoppers led the way, flinging themselves out ahead on every step. Maggie took the lead, trying to clear the brush—making it easier for David and Max to follow.

She watched the teen struggle with the stone. It slowed him down, which in turn slowed the entire group. Maggie felt an urgency, a need to speed things up even though it wasn't her journey, her destination. She offered to carry the stone for a while. The teen looked hurt and scared. He quietly and politely replied, "No thanks." His shoulders dropped as if the Arcstone had gotten heavier. She never brought it up again.

~~~ *The Quiet Earth*

"Give me your hand."

Sean slipped his hand into Maggie's and they bounded up the snowy hill. About half a foot of snow had covered the town the night before. Their footsteps marred the landscape with tiny little graves. Maggie giggled the whole time. It had been years since she was truly happy. She had been seeing Sean for several months now and their relationship was moving quickly. It had that excitement that comes with something new, and yet it seemed very familiar, very comfortable.

A small dell lay before them. They streamed down the hill toward it, leaving trails of joyful yelps wafting in the air behind them.

Maggie had mellowed over the years. The rage that pulsed inside her as a teenager had subsided. She had distanced herself from her father, from God, from anything that had let her down. Now, in her early twenties, she felt she was coming into her own. Life seemed calmer. She felt that she could actually guide this ship over less turbulent seas.

Her eyes met Sean's. A certain spirit awoke. Sean embraced her and they kissed, staving off the cold for a little bit. As they turned to continue their trek, a warbling hoot filled the air. Maggie looked in its direction to see a rather large snowy owl in a nearby tree. It was perched nearly ten feet off the ground, its dull yellow eyes focused on Sean, its full plumage specked with black here and there. She turned to Sean and grabbed his arm to steal him away. His gaze was fixed. His eyes vacant as tears began to well up. Once the bird was out of sight, he came back to, and saw her watching him. He blinked away any sign of emotion.

She led him down a path to the lake that had become still. Ice covered most of it, pockets of water dotted the center. Seagulls were scattered throughout, gently touching down on the frozen waters.

"Sean, what's going on?"

"Nothing."

"It's not nothing. Tell me. Did he talk to you?"

Sean's expression changed. His face relaxed a little, as if he felt he could share his burden.

"He said he loved me. Promised that I am not alone. That I've never been alone. He said to follow him." Maggie did not like the sound of this at all. Sean sat wearily on the snowy turf. His breathing became heavy. "I saw myself

echoing into eternity." Maggie joined him, entwined her arm with his and grasped his hand as tightly as she could.

"There is no eternity, there is only now," she began. "The past is lost. The future does not exist. Just breathe." They sat for a moment. Sean's breathing gradually slowed. Maggie picked up a small stick that had been lying nearby, covered in snow. As she held it, its frosty shell melted and flowers began to bud and bloom before their eyes. She handed it to Sean, who held his ever-so-slightly trembling hand out. He looked at it in his open palm and smiled warmly. They stood to leave, Sean gripping the twig a little too hard, such that some of the petals fell off and floated behind him.

Maggie never saw Sean again. She read in the local paper that he had returned to that same spot the next day, made his way into the lake, crashed through the ice, and been unable to make it out. A flower petal had been found in his mouth.

--- David's Story ---

"David, you never told me what this hole in your Arcstone is from." The campfire crackled in the cold night. Max sat next to David and Maggie sat across from them to complete the triangle. The boys were roughly the same age now but had little else in common. Physically Max was bigger, not taller but bulkier, more athletic. David was tall and wiry. He mostly kept to himself and spoke only when spoken to. Max always asked questions, eager to learn, but also good at getting conversations going.

“Oh, that’s nothing,” David replied, trying to avoid a discussion. Max wasn’t one to let things go. He had found that being very direct, even blunt, worked well, especially when he was younger and it still worked with Maggie. But he was smart enough to know that this wouldn’t work on David; it would just cause him to withdraw further. So he picked up a nearby stick, broke off one piece at a time and flipped them into the fire. Then he reached into his bag and grabbed a handful of berries, popped a couple into his mouth and offered some to David. David glanced quickly to make eye contact before reaching out to accept the offer.

“I didn’t mean to be rude or anything, it’s OK if you don’t want to talk about it.” There was a moment of silence while David worked through what he would say in his head before responding.

“No, it’s fine. There’s a story behind it. But let me just say first that my dad is an emotional guy. He has things that he cares deeply about. There’s a right way and a wrong way to do things. And, well, he works a lot. I mean, we have a homestead, so we have a little farm area, and some livestock—chickens and a cow and a pig—and it’s a ton of work. Basically, you spend all of spring, summer, and fall preparing for winter. And it’s like, we all help out. My mom does the cooking and cleaning and my brother and I milk the cow and gather the eggs and till the field and stuff like that, but from sunup to sundown, my dad is in the field and then at night there’s always something that needs fixing in the house.

“Well, OK, so that’s just some background. Here’s the story with the hole. I was helping my mom clean and peel potatoes. My dad called me out to help put up a new fence post. The cow kept scratching herself on the old one and uprooted it. Dad wasn't so much afraid that she would get out as coyotes or wolves would get in. He was already in a mood since this wasn't work he had planned on doing that day. He started in on me before I even got there. 'Stand up straight.' 'Pick up your feet.' Stuff like that. So we started digging a new hole, and we put the post in, but it wouldn't stand straight, so he told me to hold it while he drove it in with his sledgehammer. Usually you just tap it with the side of the hammer head until the post is steady enough that no one needs to hold it and you can take full swings at it. Well, my dad asked me to hold the post and I grabbed it with both hands and he wound up and took a full swing. I flinched and he didn't hit the top square and it kind of popped out of the ground and the sledgehammer careened to the side. This got him angry. 'What are you doing? I could have damaged the pole. Now go get it and this time hold it like a man.' I got the piece of wood, planted it back in the ground and held it again. But he said 'No, you'll drop it. Put your shoulder into it.' So I did and he wound up again and when he struck it, I could feel the tremor in my whole body. And he did it over and over with the hammer landing like an inch from my head. The stake clearly wasn't going anywhere, so I let go and started to back away. He pointed to me with the sledgehammer and told me to get back and hold it. I mumbled something like 'What's your problem?' 'What did you say?' he asked, pretty angry now. I said, 'Nothing.' 'You will address me as "sir" and you will answer me when I ask you a question.' Usually I just apologize and tell him what he wants to hear, but this time I walked away, back toward the house. He followed me so I picked up my pace and he started taking long quick angry strides after me, hammer in hand, calling out things like 'Get back here!' I ran to the house and ducked into my bedroom. He charged in after me and grabbed me by the neck. Told me that he was my father and he deserved my respect and if I wanted to live here, I better do what he says. He shoved me up against the wall and into the nightstand, knocking over my Arcstone, which had been laying on top of it. 'I'm watching you,' he said as he picked up the stone and marched out of the house into the tool shed. I followed to see what he was going to do. He grabbed a large spike, maybe a foot long, and used the sledgehammer to drive it through the stone and into the ground, basically impaling it. Then he flung the hammer at my feet and walked past me, making sure to bump me on the way back to the house. I turned around to watch him and saw my mother standing in the doorway having seen the whole thing. She didn't say a word.

"That night I snuck out of my room, pulled the spike out of the stone and left home with it under my arm."

"That's the night you began your journey? With nothing in hand but a stone? Not even a good-bye?" Max asked, his tone a mixture of pity and awe.

"Yep."

"We're glad you're here, David," offered Maggie.

By this time the fire was just a few glowing embers. They decided to call it a night and let the stars keep watch over them.

--- The Church of Life ---

They could see the cathedral now. It was immense. Even from this distance, it was imposing. The spires grew high over hundreds of acres. In the center, the largest spire grew like a horn. The shape of the church was oval with layers rippling outward.

As they drew closer and strolled among the buildings that made up the cathedral, they could see the variations in stone and texture: quartz and shale and limestone and onyx. Each piece had a personality, a history, distinct and uniquely its own. Walking near it and through it, it felt holy. Most of the buildings here used only one or two types of stone. Some types of rock were used only as decoration and not for construction. For instance, a series of statues that appeared to be made of alabaster were scattered throughout of people carrying their Arcstones. Some of the stones depicted were small and held in the palm of the hand, while others were huge and strapped to the back of the hunched-over traveler. One had a rope tied around it and the Lifer dragged it behind him. The statues had stories behind them. One depicted a girl lifting a small jagged rock high in the air with a broad smile on her face. Another a little old man clutching a smooth stone ball to his chest. Was he being protective of it? Was he ashamed? Had the stone started off sharp and craggy like the little girl's, and had he worried it until it became smooth and round? Maggie felt as if she were in a museum rather than a church.

There were few people around. A mix of tourists, worshipers, and workers. Maggie immediately took to this place. She asked David, "When is your ceremony?"

"I will register tomorrow. They will let me know then."

Max saw some workers constructing part of a wing. They were taking various stones piled high on a wagon and adding them to the wall. He went right up to them and started talking.

"Doesn't each Lifer get to place his or her own stone?"

"No, that would not be a good idea. We need to make sure each building is structurally sound and follows the plan."

"So someone designed all of this?"

"Yeah, well, not just one person, but many people over years have designed this church."

"And when will you finish?"

"Oh, it won't be finished in my lifetime. It will take many years, many lifetimes. That is, if it is ever finished."

"How does that make you feel? Isn't it unsatisfying if you can't see your work finished?"

"But there *is* satisfaction, meaning, in knowing you are contributing to something bigger. Something beyond what you yourself can do individually. My children will work on this. And so will my grandchildren. And they will improve it and use new tools and methods that I can't imagine, just as I use tools my grandfather couldn't imagine. Generation after generation. We improve."

While Max was talking, Maggie sneaked away to a corner where she could not be seen. She pulled out a small stone that she kept on a chain around her neck, no larger than an orange but lumpier and warm to the touch. She found a spot where she could wedge it into the wall, between larger stones that had been chipped and weathered. She ran her right hand over the wall, letting her fingers gently caress it. She smiled faintly and rejoined Max and David.

~~~ Separation Anxiety

"Aztok!"

No reply. She was tired of death creeping in on her from all sides. She was tired of her life being tossed around at the whims of a dull and petty God. Maggie needed to confront Him. To demand an explanation and to tell Him to stay out of her life.

They stood in her backyard. It was late at night. The skies were bright with stars. Aztok was in the form of a large falcon: proud, aggressive, ready to hunt.

"You've always been there for me? Bullshit. You're only there when you want to be. When it's convenient for you."

"You cannot demand things of me. I am your God. I do not serve you. You serve me. I created you and expect your obedience."

"Fuck you! I'm tired of this. You can't pull people out of my life like that."

"It is not for you to set limits. You cannot understand what I do and why I do it."

"I want you gone. Leave me alone."

"To reject me is to reject yourself. To reject yourself is to live without a soul. To have no soul is to live without grace. It is a fate worse than hell. You would be worse than the wicked.

"And if you deny your soul, then I shall take it back."

Aztok sprang on her. His sharp talons plunged into her torso. Maggie was frozen still, under some type of spell. He stabbed her chest with his beak, grabbing hold of something. Slowly he tugged out a dark-brown, frayed string. He pulled it, stretching his head as far away from her chest as he could, his nails still dug into her. Then he let the string drop from his beak so he could get a new grip closer to her chest. He pulled the string out again, and again, foot by foot. Maggie could only watch, not able to move, or scream or cry. It was unreal to her, as if she were watching someone else's dream. On the fourth pull, the string became stuck. Her sternum bulged with something unable to break through the pin-sized hole in her torso. Aztok pulled harder. Her skin slowly broke open, unfolding to reveal a stone a little smaller than a bowling ball, leaving raw and red flesh behind. It had a humpy and rough complexion and a ruddy brown copper-like color, and was mottled with dark splotches of black and red. The stone fell to the ground, with a sound as if it had cracked, yet it appeared fully intact. Its weight seemed immense for its size. A hundred pounds at least. Maybe two hundred. Aztok released his grip on her and flew down to pick the end of the rope up in his beak. Once he broke contact with her body she had control again, but all she could do was fall to her knees. The falcon flew skyward, away from Maggie, with his treasure in tow. She watched in silence, tired and beaten. The hole in her chest had somehow sealed itself, leaving behind two red scars—one vertical and one horizontal—and an incredible ache. Before Aztok got too far away, she saw something drop back to earth. She staggered over to it, barely able to move. Eventually she came to the spot. There was a little divot in the ground and on top of it was a piece of the stone. It was roughly the size and shape of her fist; she picked it up. Its warmth surprised her. She wondered if it was somehow alive. She knew this was the core—the other piece didn't matter.

Pocketing the stone, she turned around and began to head for home. Maggie felt different, not physically, but as if she had a different sense of self. A sense of commonality and commonness. She felt that she was a part of the earth and it was part of her. It was a oneness she had never experienced before. It was freedom and power. She was more powerful than she had ever known. And things were going to change.

--- Final Fantasy ---

A rumbling tremor rattled the windows and shook the beds. The three travelers had been put up for the night in hostel-like lodgings near the church. They had been soundly asleep until the shock wave roused them. They had no idea what had happened or why they had all woken up at exactly the same time. The three were fully alert; there was none of the sleepy hangover that sometimes accompanies waking in the middle of the night. Yet still, everything had a surreal, dreamlike quality to it. They did not know why they were awake, but they knew they were being summoned.

Instinctively they knew where to go. Max led the way. The others followed in eerie silence. Down the hall, out the door, into the musty night air they marched toward the cathedral. They did not speak to each other the entire time; for some reason they could not fully conceptualize, it was important not to break the spell.

David pushed the large metal doors open, making pinging and scraping noises that echoed throughout. They moved through the antechamber and under the arch into the main room. An immense shadow grew before the altar and started to take shape. It swirled and writhed and feathered. Wisps hardened into beaks and talons. An inky eye blinked into awareness. Aztok stood before them, over twenty-five feet tall, his head crowding the curved ceiling. The travelers halted halfway down the aisle amid the pristine pews, making sure to keep a respectful distance.

"Maggie, I realize this has all been very difficult for you. Maybe it has been too much. The pain, the losses, and now this child. You feel you have to protect him, but you're afraid you won't be able to, just as you weren't able to save Jamie, or your mother, or Sean. You were not even able to save the kittens that your pet cat had, that you and your father buried alive in a sack because you could not afford to feed them. But, you see, they are already saved. I have brought them back into my fold, into the light. We are all part of the same whole. We are all one.

Yet you have turned your back, to hide in the shadows, outside of my love. But it's OK, Maggie. I forgive you."

"What?"

"You did the best you could."

"No." Maggie started to panic, her voice started to quiver, she was overrun by conflicting emotions.

"It's time to come home, come in from the cold. Everything will be all right now."

"Stop it!" Her tears mixed with anger.

"I'm proud of you."

"That's all I ever wanted to hear." She was barely audible, barely intelligible through the crying.

"Worship me." "I will keep you safe." "I am your God." "Follow me." These phrases came from Aztok, though he wasn't speaking. They filled the air: swirling, raining down, attacking. And beneath it all, the undercurrent whispered, keeping rhythm: "Give me the boy."

Maggie let out a shrill scream. Aztok barely blinked. But then the stone blocks below his feet began to bubble up from the ground. Thick gnarly green-and-brown vines shot through the cracks. They snaked around Aztok, ensnaring him. He struggled to free himself, trying to flap his wings, but the vines only gripped tighter and tighter, the pressure building. Feathers started popping off, bits of tissue and muscle began to bulge through the few spots that weren't bound by the vines. Aztok let out a final, frail, cracked screech before bursting open. Exploding into a million pieces. No, not pieces. Birds. Thousands upon thousands of birds exploded forth, representing all kinds of species: hosts of sparrows, murders of crows, wakes of buzzards, parliaments of owls, charms of finches. They swarmed the room in a mini whirlwind before escaping through various windows and doors. Maggie and the boys closed their eyes and shielded their faces. The dust settled, and left behind, fluttering amid the now-lifeless tangle of ropy vines, was a small black bird. It hopped along feebly. Its left wing bent the wrong way, broken, dragging along on the stony ground. Maggie walked over to it, crouched down and gently picked up the bird with both hands. Max and David stood motionless, watching in stunned silence. She held Aztok close to her face, trying to make eye contact, trying to communicate her hatred, her victory, her absoluteness. She clutched him tightly now, opened her mouth, drew him in, and bit down hard. Crimson spoiled her hands and dripped to the stones below. She dropped the bloody twitching stump.

Maggie jerked back and forth violently. Her eyes became rounder, her nose and mouth joined and hardened and elongated. White and black feathers sprouted from her face and back. Her arms thinned and hollowed and plumed into wings. But the metamorphosis wouldn't complete. She remained caught in between.

She turned, looking straight at the boys, and cawed out, "God is no more. I am your future, your salvation."

Sand Castles

"Iwao, Jin, come here!" the sergeant barked. The two jumped to attention.

"Yes, sir," they both replied in unison. Iwao's posture was perfect. Jin's was less so.

"I have a mission for you two. Handed down all the way from the king himself."

"Sir?" Jin asked.

"The king wants to give a gift to the neighboring kingdom to the north. A peace offering. And since you two are the most decorated soldiers in our army, he wants you to deliver it."

"What is it, sir?" It was well known throughout the land that tensions were high between the two lands. The talks of war had led to rationing and a buildup of forces.

"This." He grabbed the round medallion hanging from Iwao's neck. "The medal of valor. This gift shows we value peace more than war."

"But sir, that is Iwao's medal, he earned it. How can he…" But Jin's protests were cut short.

"It's OK, Jin, it was the king's to give to me and it is his to do with as he pleases. It is for the greater good." Iwao's response was impassive and put an end to any debate.

"And Jin, you are responsible for this letter that goes with it. Make sure the king reads this first. Now get your shit together. You leave at noon."

"Are you ready?" Iwao stood tall with his bag slung over his broad shoulders, his short black hair matted down. Jin sat on his bunk, still packing.

"In a minute. What's the rush? It's a long journey."

"That's why we have to get moving."

They started down the road. Jin wouldn't stop talking. Iwao wouldn't start. So I guess you could say they got along well.

They traveled for days on foot before they came to the river. Unlike the others they had come across, this one had no bridge. It appeared that at one point there had been one, but all that was left now was a couple of posts and some broken pieces of wood.

"Well, now what?" Iwao asked.

"Think we can we swim it?" replied Jin.

"It looks kind of far."

"Maybe an hour's worth."

"But the current is pretty fast."

"Yeah, but we're pretty strong." Jin's grin always had that mix of mischief and confidence. It was genuine, and it made him popular with both women and men. Although some men hated it, mostly out of jealousy.

"And I don't know how to swim. In fact, I just tend to sink," Iwao confessed.

"Well, that's another matter."

They stood for a second, side by side, staring at the river, thinking in silence.

That was when it arose from the waters.

The river pulsed with waves as the giant water dragon rose and towered over them. Its head was twice the size of a man. Its teeth were sharp. Its skin a scaly bluish green. Water continued to stream down its scales as it spoke:

"The river is treacherous and you will not make it across safely without help. Let me straighten myself across the water and you can walk on my back to the other side."

Iwao and Jin stood side by side, necks slightly craned, facing the creature. Next to Iwao, Jin looked like the little brother. Make no mistake, though, Jin was not a small man by any means, but Iwao was a physical presence. Yet Iwao always deferred to Jin. For that matter, Iwao always deferred to everyone.

"And what do you want in return?" Jin asked suspiciously.

"Oh, nothing much. Just a little something to eat. Surely you must have some extra provisions you can spare. A morsel here or there," replied the dragon modestly.

"That can't be enough for a creature of your size," Jin argued.

"True, whatever food you have cannot sustain me, but many travelers need to cross this river every day, and if they each give me something, the cumulative effect is enough to get by."

"Fair enough," Jin replied. He nodded to Iwao that it was OK.

The water dragon bowed its head low and straightened its back so the two could proceed. Jin led the way, striding confidently down the backside of the beast. When the two got out of earshot of the dragon, he whispered to Iwao:

"This monster is full of crap. It will eat us once it gets the chance, so we need to be prepared. You're going to have to be the bait."

"Why am I always the bait?"

"Because you are big and slow."

"I am not slow."

"Compared to me you are," Jin said with a wink and a smile.

They walked single file for some time before they saw they were coming to an end, or rather a tail, and they still had a ways to go before they would reach the other side of the river. Iwao, now in the lead, came to a halt. Jin rose on his tiptoes so he could peer over

Iwao's left shoulder. Jin spoke. "End of the line, eh? Any second now." They both turned in unison to see the head of the beast slithering back toward them at an alarming speed.

The dragon swam toward its tail, coiling around itself. It rose from the water, exposing only its head and arms. Then it roared:

"Fools! Do you really think I live on scraps? I feed on humans and I shall feast on you both!"

"Please, spare my friend, take me instead—I am the bigger meal," Iwao offered while Jin hid behind him, making sure the dragon would not see him extracting his short sword.

"None shall be spared. You see, it is not your body I am after," breathed the vile beast, "but it is your soul I wish to devour. I just have to go through your body to get it. For I am made of the souls of those I have eaten. Each one adds to my length. And one day I will grow so big I can strangle the world."

The creature picked up Iwao with its spiny arms and webbed hands to look at him up close. The beast's breath warmed Iwao's face and blew back his hair. The stench was nauseating. "Something is wrong. Your soul is too small for your body." The dragon's eyes squinted to focus on something hidden to mortals. It peered deep, struggling to unlock the secret. Jin took this opportunity. He ducked under Iwao's dangling body and plunged the sword into the underbelly of the beast. The creature screamed, a horrific sound never before heard by man. With its free arm it reached for Jin, but Jin was too quick. In one fluid move he extracted the sword from the beast's entrails, ducked under the blow, and lopped off the beast's arm. Before it could even splash in the water, Jin cut off the dragon's other arm too. Iwao, still clenched in the lifeless fist of the dragon, now bobbed up and down in the river helplessly. The creature, blinded by pain and rage, lunged at Jin headfirst, teeth bared, ready to rend him in two. Jin leaped back, causing the demon to instead bite its own tail. Immediately Jin swung the sword down mightily, cracking open its head and slaying the beast.

Jin then fished Iwao out of the river, pulled him up onto the lifeless floating body of the water dragon. He freed Iwao from the slimy grasp of the disembodied arm. Breathless, they sat silent, soaked in a mixture of water and blood.

"Well, now what?" asked Jin, mildly imitating Iwao. The dragon's body was still mostly coiled, creating a platform that they rested on. The two of them bobbed up and down on the gentle tides. Though safe for now, they were stranded in the middle of the river. They couldn't walk back the way they came, and swimming still wasn't an option.

"We'll make a raft," replied Iwao.

Iwao pulled out his sword, measured about ten feet from the head of the dragon, and started hacking away at the body. After he had cut through, he collected the two severed arms. One he kept for himself, the other he handed to Jin. Iwao straddled the neck of the creature and Jin followed suit, sitting behind him. Using the dragon's webbed hands as oars and its neck as a raft, they paddled across the river. When they reached the other side they disembarked, leaving the giant, twisted corpse in their wake.

Trudging along the roadside, they stopped to watch an odd little display. In the near distance four men were carrying a little wooden coffin out of one of the houses. The men had gotten about a hundred paces from the house when they looked at each other with wide eyes, laid down the coffin, and opened it up. Exasperated, they quickly shut the coffin, picked it back up, and scuttled back home.

As Jin and Iwao got closer, they saw the quartet at it again, starting out of the house with the coffin in tow. So the two decided to talk to the group and see what was going on.

"Damn girl won't stay in her coffin," said the first man, middle-aged and grumpy.

"Every time we try to take her out to be buried, she somehow gets out of the coffin and ends up back in the house," said the second, a dumpy little gentleman who seemed jolly enough.

"Why do you think that is?" asked Jin.

"Well, she died in that house," replied the third—an older, balding gentleman. "She never really got out much, so she spent a lot of time there."

"Maybe she just doesn't want to leave," suggested Iwao.

"Why don't you go and ask her?" said the fourth man, tall and serious. So that is just what they did.

Iwao and Jin walked into the house while the others waited outside. Careful not to break the eerie silence, they crept in quietly. They didn't need to look far. Lying on her back in the middle of the room was the body of a little girl. They stood above her, one on either side, looking down solemnly.

"Psst. Over here," Iwao heard a voice calling from the other room. He turned and followed the voice, leaving Jin behind. Standing in the corner of the small bedroom was the ghost of the little girl. Made out of wispy smoke, she stood fully formed, with a little smile.

"Who are you?" Iwao asked as he sat cross-legged on the floor so he could meet her at eye level.

"I'm Chiyoko. Who are you?"

"I am Iwao. Why are you here, Chiyoko?"

"I live here, silly," she replied.

"No, I mean, why have you not moved on to your next life?"

"I like it here. I was only here a few years. Hardly had any chance to live at all. It's not fair. So I'm not leaving yet," she said resolutely, stomping her foot. "And you can't make me!" She crossed her arms to emphasize her stubbornness. At this point Jin had heard Iwao talking and decided to eavesdrop. He hovered outside the room and out of view while listening to Iwao talk to what seemed like no one, since Jin could not see the ghost.

"So that old wives' tale is true. The soul will not pass until the body is buried." Iwao was thinking out loud. "That's why you keep bringing it back to the house. So, if we could just…"

"You know, we have a lot in common," the ghost interrupted, taking a step closer to him. "Neither of us belongs in this world. But you are a cheater. You have help." She reached out with her right hand toward the pendant around his neck. And the closer she got, the more solid her hand became, until she was able to grasp the medallion and start to pull it toward her. "And if you were to give me this pendant, I could come back."

"I'm sorry. I cannot do that. It is not mine to give." As Iwao said this, her hand immediately turned back into smoke and the medallion slipped through her fingers, bouncing off Iwao's chest.

"Fine!" she said, pouting, and disappeared completely.

Jin waited for a moment to make sure the conversation was over before he spoke. "Iwao, what is going on? Who were you talking to?"

Before Iwao could answer, the ground began to tremble, and the floorboards started to squeak and break as roots from a tree shot up through the floor, causing Jin to lose his balance.

"Quick! Grab the body!" Iwao shouted at Jin as he started to run into the other room. The roots were wrapping around the girl's corpse, entombing her. Jin tried pulling her away while Iwao started striking at the roots with his sword. The roots were rough and barbed and cut into Jin's hands and arms. Iwao's powerful blows rent several roots in half. But this was to little avail, as for each one he cut, two more would take its place, until the girl's body was completely covered in this new, living coffin.

Tired and torn, the boys gave up.

"So now what?" Jin asked in confusion.

"Now we dig," replied Iwao.

They gathered the men from outside and all six of them began tearing up floorboards and digging up the earth beneath the house with their shovels and pickaxes. The ground quickly shifted from soil to clay and it became too hard to dig after three feet. Figuring this was good enough for their purposes, they turned their attention to the body of the girl.

They chopped and hacked at the base of the roots while leaving the girl still mummified by the bark-covered tendrils. They had to work swiftly, as more slithered toward the body, grabbing at it. With the corpse un-tethered, two of the men lifted her while the others fought back the ever-growing tendrils. Unceremoniously they dumped the little body into the shallow grave and shoveled the dirt on top as fast as they could. The ghost of the girl reappeared to make one final plea to Iwao, but she was fading too quickly and her voice was but a whisper that could not be made out over the commotion. It looked to Iwao as if she had started to cry. And when the last shovelful of dirt landed on the grave, her ethereal form blew away. The roots stopped moving, and began to petrify and crumble. The men were all sweating and panting. Jin and Iwao let out little laughs of relief. The other four were too unnerved by the situation to do much of anything. Afraid of being cursed, they recited their prayers, bowed their heads, and slunk out of the home quietly. They were followed by the two soldiers, who stood tall, proud of a job well done.

As the two groups began to split up, they shared parting words.

"You two boys headed up north?" number one asked.

"Yep," replied Jin.

"Well, be careful if you stay in uniform. We're not too welcome in that land."

"I heard any of our soldiers seen in that country is a declaration of war," said the second.

"I heard a soldier went up there to check out one of the brothels and was shot on sight," said the third.

"That's just a rumor," Jin said, trying to calm the talk. "We were sent by the king to deliver a peace offering."

"Just watch yourself," the first one reiterated.

The two groups said their good-byes and went their separate ways.

No one ever came back to that spot, a spot that had now become a shrine. The family of the girl moved away. Any others in search of land had heard the rumors and did not want to despoil the burial ground by moving the grave. To this day the land remains the same. And if you visit it, you can see the little stone marker that reads:

"May Chiyoko find the same peace here in death that she had in life."

On and on they walked. The days grew shorter. The nights grew colder. They knew they were getting closer. They could now see the smoke from the furnaces of the capital city paint little dark-gray strokes onto the bright-blue sky. It would be only a couple of days now.

Darkness surrounded them. The cold, hard rain felt like little cuts across their skin. When they came across a small opening to a cave they scrambled to seek shelter in its dark recesses.

The cave was much larger on the inside than they had thought. They trod lightly, walking only on the balls of their feet, careful not to wake any beasts that might dwell within. Softly they snaked between the stalagmites and stalactites that seemed to rise and fall before their eyes like the teeth of some enormous monster.

Once satisfied that there were no creatures lurking in the dark, they lit a fire, cooked what little food they had left, and talked.

"Iwao, when we were at the house with the little coffin, I heard you talking to someone, but there was no one there. Do you remember that?"

"Yes."

"Well? Who were you talking to?" Jin asked pointedly. He never quite knew if Iwao was shy, or quiet, or just didn't know how to talk with people. Jin often felt he had to steer the conversation, as if he were speaking with a child.

"I was talking to the ghost of the girl we buried," Iwao replied.

"What did she say?" Jin asked, trying to hide his sense of wonder with skepticism.

"She said she wanted to live again."

"Well, yeah, she would come back in some new form—unless she reached Nirvana, of course, but I doubt that. She'll probably come back as a dung beetle, the brat."

"No. She wanted to come back to life now, as the same person," Iwao corrected.

"That's crazy."

"She almost did it too. When she reached for my medallion, she started to become real."

"That's right! I did see the medallion move. But I still didn't see any girl."

"She also said something odd."

"'Cause everything else she said was completely normal," Jin joked.

Iwao continued, ignoring Jin. "She said I don't belong in this world."

"What? What does that mean?"

"I don't know. I always felt a bit different from everyone else. That I didn't quite fit in."

Jin felt uncomfortable with this conversation, so he changed topics.

"Anyway, I hear the brothels here are amazing. That's why that rumor about the soldier getting killed visiting one is so popular. *Some* say it's worth dying for. We should try one on the way back."

Now it was Iwao's turn to be uncomfortable. He had never been with a woman before. The idea of being with a prostitute did not appeal to him at all, and that that would be his first experience made it much less appealing. But he knew this set him apart. Most men, and almost all military men, went to brothels at one time or another.

"Maybe. I just want to go home, though. It's already been a long trip."

Normally Jin would have started to tease Iwao about this, but with no one around to laugh at his jokes, it just seemed wrong. He decided to change the topic again.

"So how did you earn that medal?"

"It was given to me as a reward for my bravery on the battlefield."

"I bet you leveled eighty men with one swing of your sword."

"I couldn't say."

"What do you mean?"

"I don't remember the battle."

"None of it?"

Iwao shook his head.

"Do you even remember receiving the medal?"

Iwao couldn't answer.

The two finished their dinner in silence.

As the fire burned to cinders and the cinders smoldered to ash, they lay down to rest. The wind that howled through the cave soon calmed. The cold silently gripped them, slowly seeping into their bones.

They made it inside the gates of the capital. Having explained their purpose to the guards, they received lodging inside the city walls, while word was given to the king of their arrival. They were given a room for the night at a nearby inn.

"Iwao, don't you wonder what's in this letter?" Jin asked, brandishing the note he kept close to his chest.

"Why would I? The sergeant said it was a letter to go with the peace offering."

"But how do you know? There is so much talk of war—in both kingdoms. Why would he send *soldiers* to make *peace*? Wouldn't it make more sense if it were a declaration of war? Shouldn't we look to find out?"

"No. We are only to deliver the letter."

"But what if he's sending us to death? Sending our whole kingdom to war? Shouldn't we at least know?"

"It is his job to make those decisions. It is our job to execute them. Now put the letter away."

"No, I'm going to read it. You don't have to look at it if you don't want to."

"Jin, don't."

Jin opened the envelope and read the letter within. Iwao sat watching, expressionless. After a moment Jin stopped and looked up at Iwao; his usually smiling face was sullen.

"Are you right? Is it war?" asked Iwao.

"No. It…it's about the peace offering."

"The medal?"

"It says that when you give the king your medal, you will turn to stone."

"What?"

"Iwao—*you* are the gift."

"That doesn't make sense. I've taken it off before and nothing happened."

"It was still yours, though. If you give it away, the spell breaks," Jin explained. "Did you ever hear that story about the soldier made of sand who was brought to life? That's you."

"How do you know this?"

"Everyone knows it. We just never told you."

That response sent Iwao reeling. He felt dizzy and sick to his stomach. Nothing was real.

"Iwao, are you OK?"

He didn't respond.

"Look. Let me tell you the story as I heard it." Jin let out an anxious sigh. He leaned forward, rubbed his hands together. Most tales were passed along orally, with each teller personalizing it a bit to make it their own and to play to their strengths. Jin was a natural.

“To stop the ever-encroaching tide from destroying his land, the king ordered that soldiers be fashioned out of sand to protect the shore—promising that any who survived would be granted life. So the army and the engineers and the artists went to work sculpting scores upon scores of men from the beach. They worked day and night in desperation.

“The rains came.

“It poured nonstop for weeks. The waves thrashed against the shore. The wind howled threats of annihilation. People cowered in their hovels, holding their loved ones. And when this mad season ended, and the kingdom had not been washed away into nothingness, the generals came out to inspect the coast. Entire phalanxes had been made flat, as if never there. Here and there the generals found stumps, all that remained of a few stone soldiers. With these, the generals pushed over the remaining sand and watched it crumble. They smoothed it out while thanking the soldier for his service. ‘You served bravely in defense of the kingdom.’

“After scanning miles of beach, they finally came across one who had survived. The high priests were summoned. The sacred rites were performed. The soldier stirred gently.”

Jin broke character and spoke naturally to Iwao.

“That soldier was you.”

Again, Iwao had no reaction, only silence.

“I’m sorry we never told you, but it seemed like the right thing to do. We wanted you to fit in. I’m *so* sorry. But I had no idea this was going to happen.”

Iwao didn’t believe it. He didn’t believe anything anymore.

“We should just leave. Let’s go somewhere else—to the east, maybe, where no one knows us,” pleaded Jin in desperation.

“No. We must finish our mission.”

“But Iwao, you can’t do this.”

"I must. It's what I am."

"*Who* I am," Jin corrected; his face was drowned in sadness. Iwao conceded.

"Yes. Who I am."

The next morning they arrived at the palace. The king made sure their clothes were cleaned and they were presentable. The ceremony was to take place the next day.

The ceremonial hall was full. More than full. Excitement was thick in the air. The king stood at the top of a high stone staircase. The two soldiers walked to the top while horns and trumpets and drums bellowed. When they reached one step below the king, they stopped. Jin handed him the letter. The king read it silently. He announced to the crowd that he had received a gift as a peace offering. Then he reached down to the take the medallion.

Jin watched in silent fury, his eyes fierce. Iwao was calm; his face was blank—numb. The king lifted the medal from Iwao, and immediately he became a solid stone statue. The crowd erupted into a riotous cheer. It was too much for Jin. He drew his sword and ran it through the king. The palace guards descended upon him quickly and mercilessly.

The heir to the throne stood in solemn silence. He gazed down upon the open casket containing his father. The people, his people now, wanted a response, wanted blood. As did he. Though he was only twelve, his future was clear.

The following day he destroyed the statue and declared war on the neighboring kingdom in retaliation for assassinating his father. In the speech to his subjects, he promised to raze the enemy state just as he had razed the statue of Iwao. His voice trembled at times throughout, with a mixture of sadness and rage.

The days turned into months, and the months turned into years. Many died on both sides. And not just soldiers. Villages were burned. Families were slaughtered. By the time the war was over, the boy king was now a man, and he had kept his promise—the kingdom to the south had been destroyed. And if he ever had any regret over how much blood was shed, how many lives were lost, he never showed it.

But that was ages ago. And the tides of time have swept over both these lands, smoothing them flat forevermore.

Acknowledgements

Thanks to everyone who contributed to these stories (some knowingly, some not). Thanks to my parents for supporting me. Thank you, Jennifer for inspiration, contributions (especially on Unwished and Applebite) and reading these stories and giving me honest feedback. Thanks to Kirkus Editing for helping me get this in readable form. And thanks to all the illustrators who help bring these stories to life. It was a pleasure working with each of you. (Listed in order of appearance in the book) Please check out their sites.

Dan Burgess - Cover & The Seed
http://dannybconceptartist.daportfolio.com

Shannon Toth - Unwished
http://www.illustrationweb.com/artists/ShannonToth/view

Swee Chin Foo - The Girl in the Forest
http://www.fscwasteland.net/

David Procter - Two and One
http://www.david-procter.co.uk/

Jinwoo Kim - Calimire
http://jinwoo.org

Maria Forrester - My All
http://www.mariaforrester.co.uk/

Amanda Sartor - Applebite
http://amsartor.com/

Audran Guerard - Sand Castles
http://rhinopeacock.com/

www.ingramcontent.com/pod-product-compliance
Ingram Content Group UK Ltd.
Pitfield, Milton Keynes, MK11 3LW, UK
UKHW020423250726
13967UKWH00007B/2795